阎 安 著 文世龙 译

Absolute
High Landscape

绝对高度上的风景

英汉对照

陕西师范大学出版总社 西安

图书代号　WX24N0644

图书在版编目（CIP）数据

绝对高度上的风景 = Absolute High Landscape：英汉对照 / 阎安著；文世龙译. -- 西安：陕西师范大学出版总社有限公司，2024.11. -- ISBN 978-7-5695-4494-7

Ⅰ. Ⅰ227

中国国家版本馆 CIP 数据核字第 2024VH9769 号

Absolute High Landscape

绝对高度上的风景：英汉对照

JUEDUI GAODU SHANG DE FENGJING:YING HAN DUIZHAO

阎　安　著　文世龙　译

出版统筹　刘东风
责任编辑　高　歌
责任校对　彭　燕
封面设计　孙毅超
出版发行　陕西师范大学出版总社
　　　　　（西安市长安南路 199 号　邮编 710062）
网　　址　http://www.snupg.com
印　　刷　陕西龙山海天艺术印务有限公司
开　　本　720 mm×1020 mm　1/16
印　　张　26.75
插　　页　1
字　　数　602 千
版　　次　2024 年 11 月第 1 版
印　　次　2024 年 11 月第 1 次印刷
书　　号　ISBN 978-7-5695-4494-7
定　　价　98.00 元

读者购书、书店添货或发现印刷装订问题，请与本公司营销部联系、调换。
电话：（029）85307864　85303629　传真：（029）85303879

目　录

CONTENTS

Part One *The Bird Chieftain*

Part Two *Spider*

第三辑　整理石头

第四辑　玩具城

Part Five *Absolute High Landscape*

Part Six *Ode to Wizardry*

Part Seven *The Sound of Bronze*

Part Eight *The Sea Anemone Floweret*

第七辑　青铜之音

第八辑　海葵花

第九辑　雕像与城

第十辑　对峙之美

第一辑　鸟首领

Part One　The Bird Chieftain

Giant Bird

The bird that can cover a whole big tree

Is a giant bird, a melancholy bird,

A bird that makes people scared stiff and big stones split.

The bird that can cover all the history or time

Is an owl, is a bird

That has no tongues and makes no sound.

At the top of an antique tree, the owl

Stays in ferocious silence.

An owl is a giant bird, is a patient of time,

A killer that the Space Agency

Can not control or

Give a name to.

巨鸟

能覆盖整棵大树的鸟
是巨鸟　忧伤的鸟
令人恐惧令大石分裂的鸟

能覆盖全部历史或时间
的鸟　是枭
是这种不长舌头也不发出声音的鸟
在古树的顶端　枭
恶狠狠地沉默着

枭是巨鸟　是时间患者
宇航局掌控不了
也无法命名
的杀手

Ravens

A conspiracy of ravens, a dense mass of ravens

Fly over the wilderness,

Casting shadows.

The same conspiracy of ravens

Love clamorously cawing. Flapping whooping wings, the ravens

Fly past the moon,

Casting shadows

On the moon.

A mutilated hand

Is held up, imitating the raven,

Pointing to the sky, the leaden cloth

Across which the ravens have flown.

A thicket of hair, or some seemingly hairy plant

Grows out of the earth

Like a tree.

It has an infuriated look, as though

A conspiracy of ravens were assembling in its heart

In anticipation of a next-time

Riot-like

Flight.

乌鸦

一群乌鸦　黑压压的乌鸦
在旷野上飞过
投下阴影

同样的一群乌鸦
喜欢聒噪　哗哗地振翅飞翔的乌鸦
在月亮上飞过
在月亮上
投下阴影

一只伤残之手
模仿乌鸦的样子举起来
指着天上　乌鸦飞过之后
的铅灰色的布

一丛头发　或者是类似头发的植物
长出大地
仿佛是树

它有一种被激怒的样子　仿佛
一群乌鸦正集结在它的内心

期待着下 一次

暴动般的

飞

Flight

Butterflies also fly in the dark

When darkness is hinted and allured by an over ripened apple.

" Darkness, just like a mottled dazzling beast king,

Is more capable of emphasizing the broad-day white than feeble

and gentle light."

A butterfly can also be as powerful as a malevolent bird.

When awoken, it flies booming loud in the dark

With tremendous savors of ocean tides. Like an ocean tide,

It springs out of the ocean-like motionless lurking,

Making the flight contain an intent more accurate than death.

The butterfly flying in the dark is ferocious.

It steers away from many things, but does not deliberately refuse

An unexpected bump with some other butterflies astray in flight,

And even does not refuse undue flight collisions

Ending up with an inevitable crash

Or death.

飞翔

蝴蝶也可以在黑暗中飞翔

当黑暗被一个烂熟的苹果暗示和诱惑

"黑暗就像一只斑斓夺目的兽王

比软弱而文气的光明更能强调白昼之白"

蝴蝶也可以像一只恶鸟一样有力　睡醒之后

在黑暗中带着轰鸣飞翔

带着海潮般巨大的腥味　像海潮一样

从深海般不动声色的潜伏中跳出来

使飞翔包含了比死亡更精确的意图

在黑暗中飞翔的蝴蝶是凶猛的

它绕过很多东西　但并不刻意拒绝

与另外一些迷路的蝴蝶在飞翔中

出其不意地撞击　甚至不拒绝

飞翔与飞翔过分撞击后

所导致的必然的坠落

或死

At the Heights of Eagles and Planes

My motherland is a mountainous country, many mountains
Stand in the way of many people,
Many scheduled flights have been cancelled again and again.
In the north of my motherland, my hometown,
When the chorus of animals and plants was looted off
By wild winds and times bit by bit,
When those mountains turned utterly vacant day by day,
At an early age, I already understood
People don't need a reason to bow down to mountains,
The inability to read a mountain or a range of mountains
Is nothing to be disgraced for.
I remember once I left father,
Left the man forever curved
By toil and moil by the Great Wall[1].
I walked as far as the end of road, looked up at the mountains,
At the wind vanes on the mountains, and at the higher
Lonely flight of a nameless bird and at the
Bleak blue hardly glossed over by white clouds in the sky.
When I saw the gloaming receding across the mountain ridges
And the whole world calmly fading into darkness step by step,
I couldn't help but burst out crying

As a child overpowered by curiosity and also

Overpowered by sorrow.   Then I came to learn

Some places are forbidding to people

And quite unnecessary to approach.

Towards the life beyond life

People are expected to harbor gratitude.

So not long ago, I dreamed I was attempting to desert the city.

I'd, at the heights of eagles and planes, once again experience

Those high mountains and the wind vanes on mountains,

Regretful and Remorseful.

在鹰和飞机的高度上

我的祖国是一个多山的国家　很多的山

挡住了很多的人

很多飞行计划被一再取消

在我的祖国的北方　我的故乡

当动物和植物的合唱

被狂风和岁月一丝丝地掠走

当那些山一天天变得空无一物

很小的时候我便明白

人们向山屈服不需要理由

读不懂一座山或者一片群山

不是什么丢脸的事情

我记得有一次我离开父亲

离开长城边上

那个被劳作永远弯曲的人

一直走到路的尽头　仰望那些高山

高山上的风向标　以及更高处

一只不知名的鸟的孤独的飞翔

天空白云也掩饰不住的苍凉的蓝

当我目睹黄昏擦着山脊衰落

整个世界不动声色一步步陷入黑暗

我禁不住失声哭泣起来

一个好奇心占着上风　忧伤

也占着上风的孩子　我从此懂得了

有些地方人不可以接近

也大可不必去亲近

对生活之外的生活

人应当心存感激之情

因此不久前　我梦见我正设法离开城市

我要在鹰和飞机的高度上

再次亲历那些高山　和高山上的风向标

心中充满愧疚

The Bird Chieftain

The bird chieftain lives on Qinling Mountains[2],

Lives on Kunlun Mountains[3],

Lives on the pinnacle of the Himalayas[4], an unpopulated area

With never-melting snow of thousands' years and dense fogs.

The bird chieftain is indeed high above.

Its time is all the time,

Is spring, is summer, is fall

And also is the whole winter.

Its flight takes place when deciding to experience descending.

It is that sort of landing from high to low

Then instantly starting to vertically ascend,

Rising up to a place where

Its flight is beyond sight.

Its flight is never astray from a straight line,

A flight representing mystery and

The celestial energy.

Fly over

Fly over

With chilly shadows vertically directing to throngs and the land.

Oh! It's the bird chieftain high overhead

Hard to detect in the air or on the land.

Oh ! Light and light fly!

Fly over clouds, precipices and mountain peaks!

Fly over the empty and empty scenes of transparence!

Fly over the deadly thirsty cracked lips deep in north sand seas

And the vacant north piling with thousands upon thousands of

Acres of sand seas

And the careless humans

Like ants stooping in low places

North of the north.

It is the bird chieftain

That starts to fly or land once singling out a place, declines

To descant loud in usual places, plumes itself on meditation,

Thus leaving you too far behind to emulate, and

Far too hard to narrate even slightly of it with one lifetime.

鸟首领

鸟首领居住在秦岭上
居住在昆仑山上
居住在喜马拉雅之巅　人迹罕见之处
与千年不化的雪和浓雾为伴

鸟首领确实是高高在上的
它的时间就是所有的时间
是春天，是夏天，是秋天
也是整个冬天
它的飞行是决定体验堕落的时候发生的
是那种由高向低地降落
紧接着又开始垂直高升
一直要升到望其不见之处
的飞行

它的飞行是那种始终不离开一条直线
代表着神秘和天的能量
的飞行

飞越
飞越

凉飕飕的阴影在垂直方向上指向人群、大地
那是空中和地上都难以察觉的
高高在上的鸟首领呀

那轻飘飘的飞呀
飞越云层、危崖及群峰
飞越除了空还是空的澄明之境
飞越北方沙海深处开裂的嘴唇
致命的渴
和堆积着万顷沙海的空荡荡的北方
北方之北
那蚁蝼般俯身于低矮处的
粗心的人类

那是选择好地方才事飞行或降落的
在寻常的地方拒绝歌唱　以沉思为荣
因而是你望尘莫及的
倾其一生都难以述说一二的
鸟首领

Birds Also Like Low Places

I saw birds in flight.

I believe the instinct of flight is downward.

As a fate, flight can better illustrate that

The downward instinct of things is not shameful.

Birds are also children of God.

I once closely observed birds in low places.

In low places, in a puddle of water half turbid half limpid,

Birds washed and washed the messy plumes in random,

Drank mouthfuls in random to moisten throats.

Then

A bird and another bird

Randomly pecked worms under few messy grasses

Or instead of catching worms,

Only quietly cuddled up together,

Cuddled and cuddled, expressing feelings akin,

Including those autistic birds,

They're secluded and detached, forlorn and forsaken

Just like children of human beings

Similarly pitiful.

Just as I believe in flight,

I also believe we better understand things in low places.

Apart from flight,

Birds also like low places.

鸟也喜欢低矮的地方

我见过飞行中的鸟
我相信飞行的本性是向下的
作为一种命运　飞行更能说明
事物向下的本性并不可耻
鸟们也是上帝的孩子

我曾注意观察鸟在低矮处的情景
在低处就着半浑半清的一处水潭
鸟们随意地洗濯洗濯凌乱的羽毛
随意地喝上几口润润嗓门
之后
一只鸟和另一只鸟
在几根乱草之下随意地捉捉虫儿
或者连虫儿也不捉
只是无声地挤在一起
挤了又挤　表达同类间的情意
包括那些性格孤僻的鸟
它们离群索居、形影相吊的样子
就像人类自己的孩子
同样惹人爱怜

正如我相信飞

我也相信　我们更了解低处的事情

飞行之外

鸟也喜欢低矮的地方

A Kid That Can Fly

A kid that can fly

Flies along with a black plane with black iron sheet wings,

Flies along with a big white bird with big angel-like wings.

The black plane is due to fly to an airport of the capital in north.

The big white bird is due to fly southward, fly southward

To the uninhabited Pacific Ocean.

But a kid that can fly

Resembles an aircraft that has no wings,

The navigating instrument shows no sign of his flight,

A flight having nowhere to land,

His flight like meteorites with increasing velocity

Spewing out plumes of freezing smoke

　(*But not hot steam burning down*)　.

A kid that can fly, he is enthralled in game-like crescendo flight,

His is the flight unknown to people.

The place where he's due to land

　(*a lethal landing, a landing too sudden to let out a shriek*)

Is a place unknown to people,

A place more remote and desolate than the inner heart.

一个会飞的孩子

一个会飞的孩子
和一架长着黑铁皮翅膀的黑飞机一起飞
和一只有着天使般大翅膀的大白鸟一起飞

黑飞机要飞向北方首都的机场
大白鸟要向南　向南
飞向荒无人烟的太平洋

但一个会飞的孩子
像一个飞行器一样没有翅膀
他的在导航仪上看不到的飞
没有任何地方可以降落的飞
他的像陨石一样越来越迅疾的飞
冒着阵阵寒烟
（而不是焚毁的热气）

一个会飞的孩子　他着迷于这游戏般渐入高潮的飞行
他的飞是人所不知的飞
他即将降落的地方
（致命的降落　连一声尖叫
都来不及发生的降落）

是人所不知

比内心更偏僻更荒凉的地方

Spring or Blue

The bright day tortures the moon in the sky.

The hollow blue in the sky

Tortures a helicopter.

My silence and the color of a toy hoist

Are emphasizing this spring, its desolation and brilliance

Depravation and beauty! Oh spring,

From shallow blue to deep blue to dark blue,

Seems like an assumed death.

The fate of a boy with mask stripped off is that

He is being unlimitedly dragged down into

A kind of deeper blue in deep water of a lake already abandoned

By white swans last year.

It's a kind of spring when

The helicopter frequently interrelates with the sky,

Making incessant tormented zooming sounds;

It's a kind of fate of the boy's

Containing both empathy and depravity.

But I believe this boy, whose raging body

Is calming down in the deep blue.

I believe after being put into oblivion by the worldly sleep,

His initial puzzlement and his tendency for dark blue

Are his very willing desires to be dragged down

To have himself placed in the genuine dark lake.

Down there, as if faced with the final end,

He hankers for the befall of the day

So as to ask for clean blue from the sky, for much more blue

That is denser than mayflies at the turn of spring and summer,

That is sexually thriving like a sudden outburst of blue algae,

That is prone to death but sagging

Incurably.

春天或蓝

白昼折磨着天上的月亮。
天空空虚的蓝
折磨着一架直升机
我的沉默和一架玩具起重机的颜色
强调着今年的春天，它的荒凉和鲜艳

堕落与美好！呵春天，
从浅蓝到深蓝到黑蓝，
仿佛一场假设的死亡
一个摘掉面具的男孩的命运就是
他正被无限制地拖下
一个去年就被白天鹅遗弃的湖泊
的深水

一种更深的蓝。一种由直升机
和天空频繁发生关系
而不断发出受折磨的嗡嗡声的春天
一种同时包含着同情和坠落
的属于这男孩的命运

而我相信这男孩　他的狂暴的身体

在深蓝中的平息

我相信在被尘世的睡眠遗忘之后

他曾有的困惑，他对黑蓝的倾向性

就是他要心甘情愿地拖下去

把自己置身于真正黑暗的湖泊中

在那里　像面临最后的结局

他渴望白昼降临

好向天空索取干净的蓝。更多的

比春夏之交的蜉蝣还稠密的

像突然暴发的蓝藻一样性感地勃发的

像倾向于死亡而不可救药地下垂着的

蓝

Deer or Borderland

One castle. Another one castle.

The deer in love with solitude and dashing,

North of the north, there is a place for you to go.

You pass one window, another one window,

Windows of castles.

Let her tell you and your era about that tree,

Tell you the solitary thirsty tale

Of the wilderness.

What a good tale it is!

Sleeping in nude among wild flowers and grasses,

Not yet in time to install a tiny glass pane.

The only one single little candle

Still finds no proper chamber to lighten it.

The deer in love with solitude and dashing,

North of the north, a place where wolves howl at the moon,

A good place for you to be.

Your castles wait for you,

Windows, one after another, wait for you,

The solitary wilderness and the thirsty tale wait for you,

One tree waits for you.

One castle. Another one castle.

One window. Another one window.

The deer in love with solitude and dashing,

Why don't you ever turn back?

Forward! Forward! Forward!

Even show no sign of repentance as death knocks at your door.

鹿或边地

一个城堡。又一个城堡。
爱上孤独和奔跑的鹿
北方之北有你的去处
你经过一个窗户，又一个窗户
城堡的窗户
让她给你和你的时代讲述那棵树
讲述旷野
那孤零零的口渴的故事

多好的故事呵
赤裸裸地睡在野花和草丛里
还来不及安装上一块小小的玻璃
仅有的一根小蜡烛
还找不到适合把它点亮的房间

爱上孤独和奔跑的鹿
北方之北，苍狼啸月的地方
你的好去处
你的城堡等着你
一个又一个的窗户等着你
孤零零的旷野和口渴的故事等着你

一棵树在等着你

一个城堡。又一个城堡
一个窗户。又一个窗户
爱上孤独和奔跑的鹿
你怎么从不回头
向前　向前　向前
死到临头也不显得后悔

The Tribe of Roc

The tribe of roc inhabits the deep ocean

Or a world more far-flung than the deep of the ocean.

Never before has any mankind been born and bred over there

Where plenty of giant birds and tiny birds alike occupy.

That is a place no voyages or flights can get access to,

A place no birds can reach through flight

Including the giant bird named spaceship

More titanic than roc

Save for giant birds in the tribe of roc.

Giant timbers in the roc tribe are giant ships afloat in the ocean.

Giant ships of giant timber somehow playfully float in the ocean,

Somehow leap and drop to smash an ocean unrevealed to man;

A smashed ocean somehow took flight to chase clouds and

The sky blue behind clouds like seawater ulcerated;

Then procreated are more enormous roc tribes like falcon flocks

To fly back to the tribes of roc unapproachable to man or birds;

Such are the daily routine and games of roc birds in roc tribes.

Tribes of roc with lone yet immense beauty and mystery

Act as abysses glutted with falling and hovering, and infinite

Swallowing capacity, as if a python were devouring a gigantic

Elephant in the prehistoric swampland, and after engulfing it

To satiety, began to sip the ocean with the moon immersed in,

As if the lethal emptiness would slowly gulp down everything,

The ocean would submerge deep down slowly, the whole world,

Including unknown roc tribes

Plus the unknown and known worlds delimited by

Navigators and beacons and firmly tangled up,

Would also submerge down little by little.

巨鸟部落

巨鸟部落居住在大海的深处
或者比大海深处还要深远的世界上
那里从未诞生过人类
有很多巨鸟　也有很多小鸟
那里是任何航程都不能抵达的地方
是除过巨鸟部落的巨鸟
任何鸟包括比巨鸟更巨大的
叫作宇宙飞船的巨鸟
都无法飞临的地方

巨鸟部落的巨木　漂浮在大海上就是巨轮
巨木巨轮怎样玩游戏一样漂浮大海
怎样跳起来又落下去击碎一座人所未知的大海
一座破碎的大海怎样飞起来追逐乌云
和乌云之后天空海水溃烂般的蓝
之后繁衍出类似鹰群的更大的巨鸟部落
使其重又飞回无人可及也无鸟可及的巨鸟部落
是巨鸟部落的巨鸟
日常生活和日常游戏的一部分

巨鸟部落寂寞而宏大的秘境之美

作为充满坠落和飞翔　以及无尽吞吐力的深渊

像蟒蛇在史前的荒地深处吞食着巨象

吞饱之后就开始啜饮泡着月亮的大海

仿佛致命的虚无要慢慢吞噬一切

大海会在它的深处慢慢陷进去　整个世界

包括未知的巨鸟部落

和被航海者和航标灯所划定的

未知与已知死死缠在一起的世界

也会慢慢陷进去

Notes:

[1] The Great Wall（长城）: The Great Wall of China, also called the "Ten–Thousand-li Great Wall", one of the seven wonders of the world, was listed as a World Heritage by UNESCO （联合国教科文组织） in 1987. Just like a gigantic dragon, the Great Wall winds up and down across deserts, grasslands, mountains and plateaus, stretching approximately 21,196 kilometers from east to west of China. The Great Wall is a military project built to defend against northern nomadic invaders during different periods of time in ancient China. It embodies the wisdom of ancient Chinese people and serves as a symbol of persistence and diligence as well.

With a history of about 2,700 years, some of the Great Wall sections are now in ruins or have disappeared. However, the Great Wall of China is still one of the most appealing attractions all around the world owing to its magnificent architectural grandeur and historical significance. There is a saying popular among the Chinese, "He who does not reach the Great Wall is not a true man".

[2] Qinling Mountains （秦岭）: Qinling Mountains is a geographical dividing line between Northern China and Southern China. They run west to east, stretching across Gansu Province, Shaanxi Province and Henan Province(甘肃、陕西和河南). The Qinling Mountains, mainly in northwest China's Shaanxi Province, covers more than 50,000 square kilometers and is known as China's gene bank of wild biology as it houses a huge variety of plants and wild animals. The mountain range is home to about 3,800 kinds of seed plants and 587 wild animal species, of which 112 are mammals, 418 birds, 39 reptiles and 18 amphibians. The Qinling Mountains are also home to 33 nature reserves with a combined area to the tune of 5,667 square kilometers, equivalent to one-tenth of the total area of the Qinling Mountains in Shaanxi.

[3] Kunlun Mountains （昆仑山）: The KunLun Mountains, regarded as the "ancestors of all mountains" in ancient times, span approximately 1,900

miles, running east to west （China's mountain ranges are mostly east-west oriented）, and are one of the longest mountain chains in Asia, extending across western China and the Tibetan Plateau. The climate of the Kunlun Mountain range varies according to elevation with the lower portions having cool temperate conditions, while the upper elevations close to Tibet having freezing temperatures. High winds dominate the high altitude regions of the mountain range.

【4】 The Himalayas （喜马拉雅山）: Himalaya （a Sanskrit term） means "abode of snow" because the tallest peaks of the Himalayas are always capped with snow. The Himalayas is a mountain range in Asia, separating the plains of the Indian subcontinent from the Tibetan Plateau （青藏高原）. The colossal Himalayan Mountains form a border between the Indian subcontinent and the rest of Asia. The Himalayas is also home to the world's highest peaks, with over 100 mountains exceeding 7,200 meters （23,600 feet）. Thirty of the world's highest mountains in the world can be found in the Himalayas, and to name a few, Mount Everest （珠穆朗玛峰）, Kanchenjunga （干城章嘉峰）, Makalu （马卡鲁峰）, Cho Oyu （卓奥友峰）, Dhaulagiri （道拉吉里峰）, Manaslu （马纳斯鲁峰）, Annapurna （安纳普尔纳峰） are among the significant peaks. The highest mountain in the world is Mount Everest, which reaches 8,850 meters （29,035 feet） above sea level. The freezing conditions, everlasting snow and glaciers that cover the slope create a very hostile environment for any life on Mount Everest.

Part Two　Spider

Spider（1）

Behind everything

I see spiders, I also see

Behind everything

Light and dark together wax and wane.

With water underfoot, at the roots of huge trees,

At the moment of the 20th century fading away,

Amidst the grasses and homeland I am the loneliest man.

Many a thing makes sounds while vanishing,

It forces me to speed up flowers blooming at high places.

It makes me weep and gloom while gazing.

Most times,

On the roof of a dilapidated antique cave dwelling[1],

In the damp and decayed clefts,

I am also a lonesome and desperate spider.

I weave a patch of new web hanging in the air,

I cling to it upside down

Cursing the huge saber wedged in the wall.

Most times,

The sun spins upside-down haloes around at the cave mouth.

Light appearing,

Beyond light, bugs and flies make nets for fishing.

Beyond light, I am a self-sufficient spider,

All day tasting illusions and pains,

Alongside in coexistence with the land.

蜘蛛（1）

在一切的背后
我看见了蜘蛛，我还看见
在一切的背后
光明与黑暗共同消长
水在脚下，大树的根部
在二十世纪行将就木的这一刻
众草和家园中我是最孤独的人
众多事物在消逝中发出响声
它逼迫我把花朵在高处迅速开放
它使我在观望中哭泣和忧伤

更多的时候
在一孔败荒不堪的古窑洞顶壁
在潮湿和腐朽的缝隙里
我也是一只寂寞和绝望的蜘蛛
我织成一片悬空的新网
我倒攀在那里
愤怒诅咒砌在墙中的大刀

更多的时候
太阳在窑口上旋动颠倒的晕圈

光芒莅临

光芒之外的臭虫和苍蝇设网打鱼

光芒之外我是自给自足的蜘蛛

终日饱食幻想和痛苦

与大地同在

Spider（2）

In your soul is perched a spider.

The shape of the spider is

The shape of your soul.

The way the spider spits out silk is the way that

Your soul is intricately entangled with certain phantom.

All this seems like destiny,

Also seems to be predetermined the previous life.

The spider's figure is

The figure of your soul.

Wherever you go,

The spider follows hard on your heels.

You bid adieu too many times

With too much gloom and smog-like puzzlement on your face.

You like to mingle with the crowds, trying to wipe off something

With those protruding humpbacks and swollen noses.

You're always seeking places many people frequent and vary

To ask about other spiders' whereabouts.

Given that you've not spotted the spider's shadows for long,

The spider's shadows

Are the shadows of your soul which would revive once a day,

Even are the shadows of yourself.

蜘蛛（2）

你的灵魂里盘踞着蜘蛛

蜘蛛的形状

就是你的灵魂的形状

蜘蛛抽丝的样子

就是你的灵魂与某个幻影藕断丝连的样子

这一切仿佛命运

也仿佛前世既定

蜘蛛的身影

就是你的灵魂的身影

你走到哪里

蜘蛛就能跟到哪里

你告别的次数太多了

脸上有太多的忧郁和雾霾一样的迷惘

你喜欢往人群里钻

试图让那些突出的驼背和胖鼻子帮你蹭掉点儿什么你一直在寻找

很多人离而又去变动不居的地方

去那里打听另外一些蜘蛛的下落

因为你很久不见蜘蛛的影子了

蜘蛛的影子

就是你每日都要死而复生一次的灵魂的影子

甚至就是你本身的影子

Imagine a Spider Living in a Village

Woods are flourishing.

Wild grasses are flourishing.

Wild flowers without scents, wild flowers without owners

Under the steaming sun

Are also flourishing patch after patch.

In courtyards where caves are dilapidated one after another,

Spiders are flourishing,

Spider-webs are flourishing.

And around caves wild hares and ghosts flourish even more,

In the moonlight they freely go in and out.

The peeping of red eyes in want of motives are emphasizing

The hunger of a spider in a cave dwelling,

Its steady and sure waiting,

Its non-fantasizing waiting.

A spider is destined to go hungry.

Spiders and spider-webs needing no sunshine to nourish

Are in the gloom, or in an analogously dark sequestered place.

The elaborately-designed round-plated webs

Are firmly and broadly dominating every direction

Conveying the vitality of hunger,

The vitality free from illusion and

One spider's secret of its own.

想象一只蜘蛛在村子里的生活

树林子茂盛

野草茂盛

没有香气的野花　无主的野花

在热腾腾的太阳下面

也在成片成片地茂盛

在一座又一座荒败下去的窑洞庭院里

蜘蛛茂盛

蛛网茂盛

还有窑洞四周更茂盛的野兔和野鬼

月光下它们自由出入

缺乏动机的红眼睛的窥探　强调着

一孔窑洞里的蜘蛛的饥饿

它的四平八稳的等待

它的不事幻想的等待

一只蜘蛛注定是饥饿的

不需要阳光哺育的蜘蛛和蛛网

它们在黑暗中　或类似黑暗的僻静处

那精于设计的圆盘丝网

牢固而宽广地左右着每一个方向

传达着饥饿的活力

不再幻想的活力　和只属于

一只蜘蛛的天机

The Deserted Lawnmower

A heap of iron is rusting, a machine is
Half buried in the desolate land.

The skeletons of the moon are darkly, the flight of the moon
Is the flight of an evil bird that is due to fly again tomorrow,
Replacing the poisonous thorns of roses and
The simplicity of grotesque stones.

The moon is gliding overhead the north.
The moon excretes time,
Excretes the north, the desolate land,
A heap of iron and a machine's
Destined inflammation.

The moon, an evil bird!
I'll cut the malignant tumors off your wings.
I'll some month, some year
Get back the scalpel left in the abdomen of the comet
And a truck of expired sleeping pills on the star.

The moon, an evil bird!

I'll stand in your shadows and give injections

To the north and the desolate land,

To a heap of scrap iron and a machine.

The virginity of iron is suspicious. The grease dirt is avaricious.

A machine without water to drink or grass to eat

Rusts in the north, fateful and lustful.

Ah, the deserted lawnmower!

The moon, the evil bird, will snatch you away.

Your teeth can't even gnaw on a single hair

Of the desolate land.

The skeletons of the moon, this evil bird, are darkly.

Your skeletons without water to drink or grass to eat

Are also darkly.

Deserted, deserted lawnmower!

荒凉的割草机

一堆铁在生锈　一架机器
在荒凉里埋下半截身子

月亮的骸骨是黑色的　月亮的飞行
是一只明天还要飞翔的恶鸟的飞行
代替玫瑰的毒刺和怪石的质朴

月亮掠过北方的头顶
月亮排泄出时间
排泄出北方　荒地
一堆铁　和一架机器
的宿命的炎症

月亮　一只恶鸟
我要把你翅膀上的毒瘤割掉
我要把某年某月
遗失在彗星肚皮中的手术刀
和恒星上失效的一卡车安眠药找回来

月亮　一只恶鸟
我要站在你的影子里打针

给北方和荒地
给一堆废铁和一架机器

铁的贞操是可疑的，油污是贪婪的
一架没有水喝没有草吃的机器
在北方的生锈是宿命的也是纵欲的

呵，荒凉的割草机
月亮这只恶鸟明天就要叼走你
你的牙齿已咬不住
这荒凉土地的一根毫毛

月亮这只恶鸟的骸骨是黑色的
你没有草吃没有水喝的骨架
也是黑色的

荒凉的　荒凉的割草机

In the Shadows of the World

Oh, a far far-away journey!
I'm walking in the shadows of the dales,
Walking in the shadows of the moonlight.

Along a nameless creek
With strange water-flowing sounds only the distance can have,
I'm walking in the shadows of boulders and beetling crags.

In my journey is also included a strange huge bird
With its shrieking calls and its ominous or auspicious flights
Skimming wind-like delicate shadows across the ground.

Sometimes heavy, sometimes light, fatigued, retching,
Lost in thought, occasionally humming some odd tunes,
Then uttering a long sigh to the sky, once again
Returning to the shadows.

In the shadows, I'm once again heavily wheezing,
My eyes half animal-like, half human-like
Hazy and gloomy, tender and fierce, spying on:

In the light not very far, I am hinted of my own shadows

And of the shadows of the whole world

By the shadows of some things.

在世界的阴影里

远方之远的旅程呀
我在峡谷的阴影里行走
在月光的阴影里行走

沿着一条没有名称的河流
和只有远方才有的陌生的流水声
我在一些巨石和危岩的阴影里行走

我行程中还包括一只陌生的大鸟
它尖唳的鸣叫　不知是凶是吉的飞行
让风一样精美的阴影掠过大地

时而沉重时而轻快　劳累、呕吐
若有所思　偶尔也会哼一些莫名的调子
之后对天长叹　再一次回到阴影里

在阴影里再一次粗重地喘息
我的眼神一半像动物　一半像人
迷蒙而又阴沉温柔而又凶狠地监视着：

不远处的光亮中　被一些事物的影子

所暗示出的自己的阴影
和整个世界的阴影

Accidental River

I secretly relish a place
Neither so hard as gravel or rock
Nor so hyperactive and indecisive as sand dunes,
A place where there are
A couple of dwarf trees and a meadow
Dense, neat yet not so misleading.

Just like a river coming by accident, a thin river, a river that
Replenishes in the rain after running dry in the scorching sun,
A river where the grazing horses vanish,
A river where shepherd, sheep get astray after drinking their fill,
A river where a lone wanderer loses sense of direction
Soon after drinking a mouthful of water
While crossing it.

It's a thin and cautious and seemingly humble river
Yet getting every moment ready to swell further
Or flatly perish.

偶然之河

我暗暗喜欢着一个地方
不像砾石或岩石
那样坚硬　也不像沙丘那样好动
和狐疑不定的一个地方
有几棵矮矮的树
细密　严谨　但并不令人迷惘的草地

像来自偶然之中的一条河流　细小的河流
烈日下干枯下去雨水中又涨满起来的河
是放牧的马匹消失的河
是牧者和他的羊喝饱之后迷途的河
是一个独行者越过它时
只喝了一小口
不多久就丧失了方向感的河

是一条细小和谨慎　貌似卑微
但每时每刻都准备好要再大一些
或者干脆消失的河

At the End of the Land

At the end of the land is fog,

Is the shade of a juvenile

Chased after by a lizard in the smoldering heat.

From morning till night

An ant that suffered blooded temptation

Led some other ants to

Rush elsewhere in haste.

I spied them not far on the desert

Crossing a clump of red peach blossoms and green willows

And a plot of low-lying meadow

Together with some fogs ignorant of the truth

Hurriedly perishing on the road

Leading to the end.

I'll go and collect those fogs

And white-like-fog leftovers by wolves

Like bones of sheep, horses and camels

And bones of nameless victims

As well as in those deserted factories

The scrap iron, paint pails, worn-out lathe like a penalty rack

And iron casting waste haphazardly heaped up like martyrs.

大地的尽头

大地的尽头是雾
是一个少年的影子
被闷热中的蜥蜴追逐
从早到晚
一只蚂蚁饱经血腥的诱惑
带领另外一些蚂蚁
匆匆奔赴别处

我眼看着它们　在不远处的沙漠上
越过一小丛桃红柳绿
和一块低洼处的草甸子
与一些不明真相的雾一起
急行般地消失在
通往大地尽头的道路上

我将去收藏那些雾
那些跟雾一样白的
被狼吃剩的羊骨　马骨　驼骨
和无名牺牲者的骸骨
以及那些废弃的工厂里
废弃的铁　油漆桶　行刑架似的用坏了的车床
和殉难般到处堆积的铸铁废料

The Earth is a Balloon with a Pain Inside Its Heart

Light in weight is the earth afloat in the air like a balloon,

As light as a balloon having no rind but flesh,

As light as one single breath of air

Whose amount if one extra or one less would have put one to death.

The weight of elephants, of mountains and of boulders on earth

Plus the weight of oceans in the watery ocean's depth,

The weight of whales in the basket of ocean in rocking movements

Plus the weight of a needle and the entire earth by accurate

measurements,

Oh there are people picking the light and shirking the heavy,

Treating a tiny slight load as a load super heavy.

In fact, the comparison between heavy and light, or

The relationship between light and heavy is simply a matter of

One breath of air, a matter of one breath of air named oxygen

And is an art of showing the outcome within three or five minutes.

A man is living in the world.

A bird is flying in the sky.

Plus a plane is floating above clouds or below clouds.

Are you a man who behaves well?

Are you a tree that behaves well?

Are you a bird that behaves well?

Is it that you are ignorant of that very pain in the heart of the earth,

Light or heavy,

But the earth floating in the air like a balloon is aware of it.

The earth is a decent planet floating like a balloon,

Well versed in the art of lightness, in the art of one breath of air.

It has a pain hurting its heart, has bitterness teeming its belly

And a belly of salt pickling wounds, whose weight equals the ocean

But never lets it out to those who can't tell light from heavy.

It once experienced

The weight of a balloon with a pain inside its heart

And the weight of the earth as light as that of a balloon,

Which can only be measured by a balloon.

Ordinary people don't figure it out

Nor does it speak it out.

地球是一颗心里有痛的气球

像气球一样在空气里飘着的地球是轻的

轻得就像一只有瓤无皮的气球

轻得就像一口气

多一口少一口就能要人命的气

地球上大象的重　　山脉的重　　巨石的重

包括湿淋淋的大海深处

大海的重　　大海的篮子摇晃着的鲸鱼的重

包括那些能精确算计　　一根针的重

和整个地球的重　　拈轻怕重

把一丝丝的重也看得重如千钧的人

其实重与轻　　轻重之间

都是一口气的事情

都是一口名叫氧气的气

在三五分钟内见分晓的艺术

一个人在世上活着

一只鸟在天上飞着

包括一架飞机

是在云层之上还是云层之下飘浮

你是不是一个检点的人

你是不是一棵检点的树
你是不是一只检点的鸟
是不是地球心里那份不知轻重的痛
也许你自己不知道
但气球一样在空气里飘着的地球知道

地球是一颗气球一样飘浮着的好星球
它精通轻的艺术　一口气的艺术
心里有痛　有一肚子苦水
有一肚子大海那么多的腌着伤口的盐的重
也不说给那些轻重不分的人

它曾经经历的
属于一颗心里有痛的气球的重
和只有气球才能衡量出的
与气球同样轻的地球的重
一般人看不出来
它也不说出来

Sleeping With the Mirror

A white swan
  (*Perhaps merely something analogously white*)
Together with its unreal white,
In the Heavenly Lake[2] in autumn,
In a place more remote than Sinkiang,
Is sleeping with the mirror.

One curved megalith with its black lichen
And a big heap of deadly white bird dung,
On the steep crags high over the mighty river,
In the winds of the ancient times, under the wings of
A bird attempting to ascertain its flying posture,
Is sleeping with the time.

A snake that shed its white skin in the jungle
  (*All this is merely in the imagination*)
Is chasing a starving tiger but in vain.
After losing its way back to its lair,
It flees in panic.
Before dark it must hurry to the moors
And sleep with the dark clouds and the moon.

My father, with his gray hairs

And white bones in his black skin,

Tonight in my hometown's dream and my dream,

Shining whitening cold light with nowhere to place

And with certain indescribable gloom,

Is sleeping with mountains in the north.

和镜子睡在一起

一只白天鹅

（也许仅仅是一个类似的白乎乎的事物）

和它的不太真实的白

在秋天的天池里

在比新疆还远的地方

和镜子睡在一起

一块有弯度的巨石和它的黑青苔

和一大堆白花花的鸟粪

在大河上空的危崖上

在古代的风中　在一只试图确定

飞翔姿态的鸟的翼翅下

和时间睡在一起

一条蛇在丛林中蜕掉白皮

（这一切只是在想象之中）

追逐一只饥饿的老虎未果

在迷失了返回洞穴的道路之后

由于恐惧而仓皇逃窜

天黑之前它要赶到旷野上

和乌云　月亮睡在一起

我父亲和他的白发

以及他的黑皮中的白骨

今夜在故乡的梦中和我的梦中

闪着无处安放的白花花的寒光

和某种难以名状的忧伤

和北方的群山睡在一起

The Sun is Burrowing Somewhere

The sun is cozily warm
Behind me, and behind a porcelain that is lazing time away;
Inside the color that seemed already outdated last year,
The sun is burrowing.

Behind a wall, deep in the lush growth of weeds,
The sun, in partnership with a full-dappled female serpent
And five or six raw eggs it just stole,
They are together burrowing.

Behind summer, behind a half red half green pomegranate,
Sometimes in the core of flower pedicle just closed up,
The bountiful sunshine makes a colored caterpillar exhilarated,
Makes a colored caterpillar also in partnership with the sun
Set about burrowing there.

When loneliness expands upward, a goshawk
Is also in the air flapping its wings.
Behind a goshawk,
Behind its ferocious swift flying shadows,
In the dazzling white dizzy center of the sky

The sun is burrowing there.

太阳在什么地方打地洞

太阳暖洋洋的
在我的背后　和一件消磨着时光的瓷器的背后
在去年就显得陈旧的颜色里
太阳在打地洞

在一堵墙的背后　杂草茂盛的深处
太阳伙同一条浑身花斑的母蛇
以及它刚刚偷来的五六只鲜蛋
它们在一起打地洞

在夏天的背后　在一颗半红半绿的石榴的背后
有时是在刚刚收敛的花蒂的中心
充足的阳光让一条花毛虫也欢欣鼓舞
让一条花毛虫也能伙同太阳
开始在那里打地洞

寂寞向上扩张的时候　一只苍鹰
也在空中鼓动双翼
在一只苍鹰的背后　在它的凶悍
而疾厉飞行的影子的背后
在天空白花花的晕眩的中心

太阳在那里打地洞

Notes:

【1】Cave dwelling（窑洞）: Cave dwelling（cave house or cave）is a traditional architectural form in the northern part of Shaanxi province, which is mostly loess plateau, an ideal environment for the development of cave dwellings. The most representative cave dwellings are located in the northern area of Shaanxi Province, especially in Yan'an and Yulin districts（延安和榆林地区）, where cave dwellings can be seen everywhere.

Loess in plateau is sticky, hard and not easy to collapse. People living on the Loess Plateau of northern Shaanxi have been dwelling in cave houses since 4,000 years ago. Most caves dwellings are carved out of the mountains. Local villagers carve caves in a simple, cheap way. What's more, cave dwellings are easy to heat in winter and cool in summer. Today, cave dwellings are still widely spread on the loess plateau with more than 40 million residents.

The natural-style cave dwellings in the loess region display the principles of harmonious coexistence of humans with nature, the simplicity of construction designs, and frugality in use of material. The architecture itself is also sturdy and durable, and since it is very comfortable to live in, it is widely used by the local people of the day.

【2】Heavenly Lake（天池）: Heavenly Lake is a small mountain lake in Tianshan Tianchi National Park（天山天池国家地质公园）, a high mountain area similar to the Alps（阿尔卑斯山）. The surrounding snow-capped peaks are magnificent. The lake is a summer resort popular with tourists, with spruce trees all around. The lake itself is about 3 kilometers long and averages about 600 or 700 meters wide （about 2 miles by less than half a mile）. The lake surface is shaped like a half-moon and at its deepest point the water is about 100 meters （328 feet） deep. The clean blue lake is quietly tucked away among the mountains. It is surrounded by many rugged and forested valleys leading down from nearby peaks, which reach about 2,400 meters （7,800 feet） in altitude. Surrounded by mountains, trees and flowers, and silhouetted against the blue sky, the Heavenly Lake is simply beautiful.

It is best to visit the Heavenly Lake in the late spring, summer or early fall, when it's not so cold. Temperature differences in Urumqi（乌鲁木齐） between morning and evening are large. Even in summer, there may be frost in the early mornings. Tourists should bring a coat.

Yurts（蒙古包） have electricity and wood- or coal-stoves. You won't feel cold in them, but winter is still not recommended. The region is dangerously cold in winter.

第三辑　整理石头

Part Three　Sorting Out Stones

Post Office

Exceptionally good fruits are all placed on the patio;

Plus you, the very berries from deep in the old-growth forest,

Perpetually yearned for by a certain animal

Named sheep,

Are also placed on the patio. It's summer season.

Being slightly high matters little.

Being slightly eye-catching matters little.

I only have a melancholy cement patio

That will presumably disappear.

Yet the sun, water and

Treacherous winds will appear,

Thunders and meteors will appear.

Restless friends are talking confidentially

Of another gathering

After summer.

My cement patio is aloft.

Look down! All the people crazed about plundering,

The people haunted by illness and busyness,

The people in chorus kicking up dust and din,

Some are kith and kin, others are enemy and foe.

The patio, fruits, summer

And one gathering of us

Are things over their heads.

How in the end the fruits got totally consumed,

A chaotic crowd, all nattering and chattering!

How come they ended up in discord is not important.

It's solely a gathering between friends after all.

There is only one sentence that makes some sense:

"The post office is the hub of the world.

We are the letters

Being hurriedly sent elsewhere by someone."

邮政局

好样的水果都搬到阳台上
还有你这来自老森林深处
被一种叫作羊的动物永久梦想
的浆果
也搬到阳台上　夏天了
高一点不要紧
显眼一点不要紧

我只有忧郁的水泥阳台
也许还将失去
但是太阳，水和
叛逆的风会来
雷电和流星会来
不安分的朋友们密议
夏天之后
的另一场聚会

我的水泥阳台在高处
向下看　一切热衷于攫取的人
被疾病和忙碌运作的人
激起尘土与噪音合唱的人

有的是亲人　有的是仇人
阳台　果实　夏天
还有我们的一次聚会
是他们头顶上的事物

果实最后被怎样享用殆尽
一群人　七嘴八舌
最后怎样不欢而散都不重要
这只是一次朋友的聚会

只是有一句话挺有意思：

"邮政局，全世界的核心
我们是谁发出的信件
正被匆匆寄往别处。"

Glass

Glass falls to the ground, in pieces,

In numerous shapes,

The shapes of death.

Fragile glass—Beware!

(*It has no heart.*)

Closely observe a heap of broken glass,

The jagged edges are the shapes of death.

The world is dull and monotonous.

There is nothing fun to play with,

Let alone playing with broken glass.

For the shapes of broken glass

Are the shapes of death.

玻璃

碎玻璃落了一地　碎玻璃
数不清的形状
就是死亡的形状

玻璃这种事物　你可要小心
（它没有心脏）
仔细观察一堆碎玻璃
除了死亡的形状　还是死亡的形状

世界枯燥乏味
没有什么好玩的　也不要玩碎玻璃
因为碎玻璃的形状
就是死亡的形状

The Death of the Window Washer

He loves glass, this joyful window washer.

Trucks and trucks of glass, glittering,

Are transported by him to every corner of the city.

I remember, and the whole city remember

He has a childish expression, and every day

Looks at the blurred beauty of the world from behind the glass.

I remember, at noon that day

When the street and the whole truck collapsed all at once,

When glass at his bosom and he himself shattered all at once,

Death befell too soon to escape.

He did not shriek,

The joyful window washer did not shriek.

For that moment, he did not shriek.

The window washer known far and wide, a rustic swain,

Was all smiles every day.

For that moment, he did not shriek, but I'd rather believe

For that moment, he was felicitating himself that

He'd enter the dream hereafter—

He dreamed: *Vales and white fogs reappear in the distance.*

In the vast world, beauty exists after all:

A sleeping white bird embraces a fiery red heart

（*But not the shattering in the wake of a heavy falling*）．

清洁工之死

他爱玻璃　这个快乐的清洁工
整车整车的玻璃　闪光
被他押送到城市的各处
我记得　整座城市也记得
他有一副孩子的表情　每天都在
玻璃后面看世界的模糊之美

我记得那天正午时刻
当大街与整辆卡车同时陷落
当他怀抱的玻璃与他同时碎裂　死亡猝不及防
他没有尖叫
快乐的清洁工他没有尖叫

那一刻他没有尖叫

远近闻名的清洁工　乡下来的孩子
整天笑眯眯的
那一刻他没有尖叫　而我宁愿相信

那一刻，他正庆幸自己从此进入了梦境——

他梦见：山谷和白雾又在远方呈现

世界之大，美总归有
一只睡眠的白鸟怀抱着火红的心脏
（而不是重重地降落后的破碎）

Two Cleaners

Two cleaners are underground,
In the sewers washing a city.
There they eat, sleep and even bear children.
Even as alike as the city people, they
Sometimes are happy, sometimes they worry.

Somewhat absurd!   The two cleaners
They couldn't cleanse this world, tormented and fatigued,
So came travelling stained in dust from afar
Only aiming to come straight at me just for pleasure.

Lo! In the morning, once getting off the train,
Too hasty to inform me, they headed straight for my bedroom,
Disturbing the good dream of a lazybones
In another city without repair for long years.

The two cleaners, they tried in vain to find me,
Only to find a ball of used string for binding things and
An old coat faded for missing the old times,
My sole legacy.

The two cleaners, pals of mine

They couldn't find me,

Couldn't find the faucet,

Left resentful.

两个清洗工

两个清洗工　在下面
在下水道里清洗一座城市
他们在那里吃饭、睡觉甚至生儿育女
甚至和城里人一模一样地
或而幸福或而烦恼

这有点荒唐　两个清洗工
他们洗不干净这个世界　又苦又累
就风尘仆仆从远方赶来
就想冲着我来过过瘾

这不早晨他们刚走下火车
来不及打招呼就直奔我的卧室
惊扰了懒虫的一场好梦
另一座年久失修的城市

两个清洗工　他们找不到我
只找到一团绑过东西的旧绳索
一件因为怀念往昔而褪色的旧衣服
我唯一的遗产

两个清洗工　我的朋友

他们找不到我

也找不到水龙头

悻悻而归

A Morning That Can't Be Given a Name to

Early morning, they start off
In the direction of the horizon. Early morning,
The people walking like in a dream,
The people going farther and farther from the village,
The people still within sight when seen
From one highest City Tower

The people making the desolation and the north have chances
To further extend and expand,
Seem to be talking about certain interesting subject,
Walking farther and farther away

Talking regardless of others around.
The people walking forward obstinately like the fog,
The people seemingly acquaintances yet strangers,
The people going somewhere with unknown intentions,
Set me heart-thumping with some uneasiness.

Being in the dark, the dark hard for a full-length view,
I really find it hard to give a name to this morning.
This throng of people walking farther and farther,

I guess, maybe they are talking about a spider,

A spider swimming in the soil like a fish.

But what place are they heading for?

What's their intent for going there?

I have no idea.

Maybe, heaven knows!

Like a spider, I am

Merely an onlooker hiding in the dark,

Intoxicated in looking into the distance

But not fond of giving names.

I am only a person who adores the solitude superior to death.

一个无法命名的早晨

一大早就出发了
向着地平线　一大早
这些如同梦中行走的人
离村庄越来越远的人
在一座最高的城楼上
还能望见的人

这些让荒凉和北方有机会表现
得更为博大的人
仿佛在谈论着什么有意思的话题
越走越远

旁若无人地谈论着
这些雾一样执拗地向前走的人
这些看似眼熟而又陌生的人
不明用意地要去一个地方的人
让我有些不安　心里怦怦地跳

由于在暗处　看得不太全面
的暗处
这个早晨我的确难以命名

这群越走越远的人
我猜想他们或许是在谈论一只蜘蛛
一只鱼一样在土里游泳的蜘蛛
但他们要去什么地方
他们要去那地方的意图
我不知道

也许天知道

像蜘蛛一样　我
仅仅是一个躲在暗处的旁观者
沉醉于远而又远的观看
但不喜欢命名

我仅仅是一个热爱那种高于死亡的独处的人

The Diggers in the Suburbs

Ask the stars to descend
To shine upon the figures in the dark,
The diggers leaving home early and returning late,
Leaving no trace
And making no voice.

The diggers who, at the peep of dawn
In the absence of people's notice,
Slip back into the day and deep into life.

Ask the stars to descend to shine upon
The up-to-down dim glints of sharp tools, upon
The scenes of the land's warm heart being pierced through,
Upon stones and a place deeper than stones,
Another world dominated by silence,
The silence more cunning than stones.

Ask the stars to descend,
I'll sure remain silent. I am
Merely an observer,
An observer whose eyes, like stars

Brilliant and distant.

An observer whose eyes, like stars

Obscure and curious.

Ask the stars to continue

To shine upon the diggers working in secrecy,

The people who next time in the dark

Will resume digging into the depths

But will decline to voice it in public.

郊外的挖掘者

请求星空下垂
照耀这些黑暗中的身影
这些早出晚归
不留任何痕迹
也没有传出任何风声
的挖掘者

这些天一亮　趁人们不注意
悄悄潜回白天
和生活深处的挖掘者

请求星空下垂　照耀那些自上而下
的锐器上幽暗的闪亮
土地温暖的心腹被穿透时的情景
石头　比石头还要深的地方
比石头还要诡谲的沉默
这些沉默控制着的另一个世界

请求星空下垂
我肯定会不吭声　我
仅仅是个观察者

眼睛像星星一样又亮又远
的观察者
眼睛像星星一样迷惘
而又好奇的观察者

请求星空继续照耀这些
秘而不宣的挖掘者
这些在下一次的黑暗中
还要继续向深处挖掘
但拒不声张的人

The Man Drilling a Water Well by the Seashore

The man drilling a water well by the seashore

Is a haggard person, a somber person.

Familiar with straits, dumb-headed seabirds and even sea devils,

Sometimes he lives with them on hills,

Sometimes he lives alone on rocks,

Sometimes he, in the fishing moratorium, lives

On the toppling mast that overlooks the whole sea.

The sea looks like a blue wasteland

Surrounded by white waves and white seabirds' mournful cries.

All the white birds hover over the sea,

All the black birds hover in the sky,

The man drilling a water well by the seashore,

Like a huge spider, uses fishing-nets

To dangle himself on the toppling mast.

Like a seabird many times broken-winged by the sea,

The man drilling a water well by the seashore,

He is well versed with the secrets of the sea,

His little water-well is so delicate, so

Crystal that all people coming to sea want to drink from it, a fish

Pregnant long yet incapable of spawning wants to drink from it,

The whole sea that is dying of thirst

Also wants to drink from it.

在大海边上打水井的人

在大海边上打水井的人
是个憔悴的人　阴郁的人
他熟悉海岬、笨海鸟甚至海鬼
有时他和它们一同住在山上
有时他独自住在礁石上
有时他住在休渔期
可以俯瞰整座大海的摇摇欲坠的桅杆上

大海仿佛蔚蓝色的荒地
簇拥着白色海浪和白海鸟哀婉的鸣叫
所有白色的鸟都在大海上飞
所有黑色的鸟都在天空中飞
在大海边上打水井的人
像一只巨大的蜘蛛　用渔网
把自己悬挂在摇摇欲坠的桅杆上

像一只已经多次遭遇过大海折翅的海鸟
在大海边上打水井的人
他是如此深谙海水的秘密
他的小小的水井如此精致
如此清澈　所有前来看海的人要喝它

一条怀孕已久却无法产卵的鱼要喝它

快要渴死的整座大海

也要喝它

The Man Snatching Lightnings Barehanded

Many friends are doomed to depart,

Many things are doomed to disappear,

Just as we're doomed to see dust and ashes,

Just like cloud shadows and broad-leaved epiphyllum[1].

Just like a man snatching lightnings barehanded,

Just like the grey mane of a wolf

Running in the wilds,

Running on mountain ridges,

In the dim twilight or in the broad daylight.

As if a certain illusion flicking by,

Just like stones falling along with the cataract,

Sparkling in white gleams of spraying waterfalls,

The man snatching lightnings barehanded

Beat down many trees,

Beat down many mountains,

Held many rivers in his hands just like holding a handle,

Just like holding a whip.

The man lashing us with a whip,

The man lashing trees and mountains and fields,

The man lashing the heavy-headed and light-footed savages,

The man snatching lightnings barehanded,

Is the man waiting for us to capture ghost figures

Of our own and of the world,

As if capturing bears

Out of the shadows.

徒手搏取闪电的人

很多朋友注定要离开

很多事物注定要失踪

就像我们注定要见到尘埃和灰烬

就像云影和昙花

就像徒手搏取闪电的人

就像狼的灰色的鬃毛

在旷野上奔走

在山脊中奔走

在黯淡的暮色中或光天化日之下

仿佛某种幻觉一闪而过

就像随着瀑布跌落下来的石头

在瀑布飞溅的白光中闪闪烁烁

徒手搏取闪电的人

很多树被他打倒了

很多山被他打倒了

很多河流像把柄一样被他握在手里

就像握着鞭子

用鞭子抽打我们的人

抽打树和山野的人

抽打头重脚轻的毛野人的人

那个徒手搏取闪电的人

是等着我们从影子里

捕熊一样捕捉

自己的和世界的

鬼影子的人

Sorting Out Stones

I once saw a man sorting out stones,

A man bent over a pile of stones, with his back to others,

A man, like a rooster, in a rough and big voice,

Shouting all alone at the stones all day.

Stones are taken out of mountains,

Carried out of the stone quarry piece by piece.

Must sort them out piece by piece,

Must let the stones' orderly and upright rhythms

Emerge sonorous and dignified

So as to erase the wounded marks left by iron-killings.

A somewhat low man for a slight humpback

Is a man wholeheartedly sorting out stones.

Time and time again, he fondles

The stones that are sorted out again after lethally wounded.

I even saw with my own eyes how he

Eyed his shadows on the lofty huge stone walls,

Concentrated and contented,

As if experiencing an abrupt encounter with a long-lost friend.

I saw the man sorting out stones,

A man slightly cold at first sight, a man like a prisoner,

Who made things produce extraordinary sounds

But content in his silence,

A man who piled up stones piece by piece

Producing symphony-like magnificent rhythms,

A man who has stone-like rigid textures

And refined streaks.

The man I saw sorting out stones, I mean

I'd rather believe you have also seen him

And even believe that certain day certain month certain year

You used to be the man sorting out stones,

You are the very man sorting out stones.

整理石头

我见到过一个整理石头的人
一个人埋身在石头堆里　背对着众人
一个人像公鸡一样　粗喉咙大嗓门
整天对着石头独自嚷嚷

石头从山中取出来
从采石场一块块地运出来
必须一块块地进行整理
必须让属于石头的整齐而磊落的节奏
高亢而端庄地显现出来
从而抹去它曾被铁杀伤的痕迹

一个因微微有些驼背而显得低沉的人
是全心全意整理石头的人
一遍遍地　他抚摸着
那些杀伤后重又整好的石头
我甚至目睹过他怎样
借助磊磊巨石之墙端详自己的影子
神情那样专注而满足
仿佛是与一位失散多年的老友猝然相遇

我见到过整理石头的人

一个乍看上去有点冷漠的人　一个囚徒般

把事物弄出不寻常的声响

而自己却安于缄默的人

一个把一块块的石头垒起来

垒出交响曲一样宏大节奏的人

一个像石头一样具有执着气质

和精细纹理的人

我见到过的整理石头的人

我宁愿相信你也见过

甚至相信　某年某月某日

你曾是那个整理石头的人

你就是那个整理石头的人

Messenger's Hymns

In the branch-shaped firelight of lightning,

He walks

Yelling and shouting,

Somewhat exhilarated like an upcoming storm.

I understand this lad,

The lad fond of travelling.

He just brought back a bouquet from afar.

In spring,

Earlier in sleet, he was an apprentice at the blacksmith's,

Composing hymns while striking spraying fire sparks:

"Spring delivers bliss between the sea and the clouds.

While in summer, pistils of stars, like burning,

Cast a ruddy glow in the whole firmament.

The huge plate of the sky is sagging, like mother's belly,

Not only getting close to the life but composing the life itself.

A bird skims over a garden that is trying to awaken in the rain,

Whisks by my arm, singing,

Flying elsewhere more mirthful."

The branch-shaped lightning firelight is
Over the dense shade of summer
Ahead of him.

Oh! The solely loner lad fond of beauty!
I understand him.

The peace and kindness he ever used to have
Come from the suppression of the gales of life.
But he heartily loves—
The genuine gales and even
The burning fire though reverberating throughout the zenith.

The messenger-like clear face
Flickers in the lightning-illuminated suburbs.
At the moment, in a genuinely unpopulated place,
He wants to conceal all his afflictions in the rainstorm.

使者的赞美诗

在雷电枝形的火光下
他行走着
大喊大叫
与即将来临的暴风雨一样有点兴奋

我了解这孩子
这个爱旅行的孩子

他刚刚从远方带回花束
春天
更早时候一个雨雪天气，他是铁匠铺的学徒
一边打击着飞溅的火星，一边写赞美诗：

"春天在大海和云朵之间运送幸福
而夏天，星星的花蕊烧红了全部苍穹
天空硕大的葵盘下垂着，像母亲的肚皮
不仅接近了生活而且构成了生活本身

一只鸟掠过一座雨水中试图觉醒的花园
掠过我的手臂和歌唱之间
飞往更加热闹的别处。"

雷电枝形的火光

在夏天的浓荫之上

在他的前方

爱美的独来独往的孩子呵

我了解他

他曾经的平静和蔼

来自对生活狂风的平息

但他真心地喜欢着——

真正的狂风

和哪怕是响彻天顶的熊熊烈火

使者般清亮的面孔

在雷电照彻的郊外或明或灭

此刻，真正的无人之境

他要把全部的痛苦隐藏在暴风雨中

Notes:

【1】 Epiphyllum（昙花）：Epiphyllum, from the Greek, meaning "upon the leaf"（which does not grow from a branch but from the edge of a leaf） can be grown in the ground or in leaf litter on the branches of trees, and is also easy to grow in large hanging basket or supported in a large pot with stakes or trellis.

Epiphyllum refers to any cactus of the genus epiphyllum having flattened jointed irregularly branching stems and showy tubular flowers. The broad-leaved epiphyllum, which also goes by the names of orchid cactus （a misnomer as they are unrelated to orchids） , the beauty under the moonlight （月下美人） and night-blooming cereus, is a beautiful, precious and strongly fragrant starburst- shaped white flower which usually blooms at night, and its blossom only lasts but one night, that is to say, is wilted with the first rays of the morning sun. According to a Buddhist legend, the plant blooms only on the birth of divine kings.

Broad-leaved epiphyllum, which blooms for a very brief period, is often used by philosophers and poets to describe life as a flash in the pan, "Life is a longitudinal fleeting meteor, like broad-leaved epiphyllum, in a blink of an eye, it would disappear in the night sky and the universe" .

第四辑　玩具城

Part Four　The City of Toys

The Darkness

The entire room of darkness is asleep
Beside mother, and
Under her red cloth.

The entire world of darkness is asleep
Beside mother, and
Under her window.

The entire sky of stars are also asleep
In the dark, making deafening snores all around
Like crickets and grasshoppers.

In the dark, mother alone is awake,
Her hand affectionately caressing
The darkness around, which needs a lamp
To brighten.

The darkness is also a child, mother says.
God is dead,
The darkness needs someone to keep an eye upon.

黑暗

满屋子的黑暗都睡着了
在母亲　和她
的红布下

满世界的黑暗都睡着了
在母亲　和她
的窗户下

满天的星星也都睡着了
黑暗中　发出蟋蟀和蚱蜢
震响四野的鼾声

黑暗中　只有母亲醒着
她的手掌亲切地抚摸着
四周的黑暗　需要一盏灯
点亮的黑暗

黑暗也是一个孩子　母亲说
上帝死了
黑暗需要人的照看

Tonight, I Cry

Tonight, I cry!

The starry sky thus takes on strange beauty.

With my elbows,

I hoist this ghastly pale silence

In the pale humble abode.

I can see everything

Yet I wish not to see anything at all.

In the dark

The world appears super huge,

I pray not to hear anything at all.

Yet somewhere quite near my head,

In the electric ballast

Electric currents are buzzing while passing through.

The electric currents are transmitting pale nutrition

To the pale electric bulb,

Just like the pale humble abode

In the deep still night

Highlighting my pale thoughts.

Tonight, I cry!

The starry sky thus takes on strange beauty,

Such strange beauty.

今宵，我哭泣

今宵，我哭泣
星空为此而美丽

我用肘子
托起惨白的陋室里
这方惨白的沉寂
我能看得见一切
我一切都不希望看见
黑暗中
世界显得很大
我祈求不要听见什么

而在我头脑很近的地方
在镇流器里
电流经过时在响
电流在给惨白的灯管
输送惨白的营养
正像惨白的陋室
在这静夜深处
烘托着我惨白的思想

今宵，我哭泣

星空为此而美丽

异　常　美　丽

Fog

The fog is unfolding its black claws.

The fog is running. In the body of the fog,
The city is as robust as a man of virtue.
The mice conveying ashes and drugs
Grimace in the fog,
Trotting by in haste.

The fog is the egg laid by the city.
The claws of the fog, frail claws,
Fail to lacerate the face of the city.

雾

雾张开黑色的爪子

雾在奔跑　雾的身体中
城市健壮得像个君子
运送灰烬和毒品的老鼠
在雾中扮扮鬼脸
一溜烟小跑而过

雾是城市下的蛋
雾的爪子　软弱的爪子
抓不破城市的脸

Spring

I mean, in the spring of this year,

Rains in affluence and flowers in radiance.

Flowers bloom in all their glory.

Flowers with no name also bloom with fame far and near.

Gee! Rains in extreme affluence!

Flowers in extreme radiance!

春天

我说的是今年的春天
雨水好花也开得好

花开得真好
没有名声的花也开得远近闻名

啊呀！雨水真好
花真好

The Lark is Chanting

The lark is chanting.
The lark actually is all along chanting.

As we're steeped in deep meditation in the gloom,
Abruptly, in the meadow ahead it's a lark
Alone roaming along.
She strolls straight up with grace and ease
Beaming at us, the lark
Showing plump teeth, more glossy than pearls.

The lark is chanting.
The lark actually is now and then in the distance,
In the sky light or in the clouds
In flower petals or in succulent grass
Chanting.

The lark is actually just among us.

In places we stir up something flighty and light,
She holds her proud and charming face high.
In places she passes, things are wholly bathed in light,

Fragrance surging as a tide,

Birds and beasts holding breath in silence.

The lark, my red-mouthed and white-toothed sister!

She is, with her back to the mundane world, chanting.

She is in the mundane world chanting.

She, with her chanting paws,

Tightens her grip of me, of my sinking heart and

The sinking world.

The lark is chanting.

百灵子在歌唱

百灵子在歌唱
百灵子，其实一直在歌唱

当我们在昏暗中俯首沉思
蓦然间前方的草坪上就是
百灵子正独自漫步
她大大方方地迎面走来
对着我们微笑　百灵子
牙齿饱满，比珍珠还晶亮

百灵子在歌唱
百灵子　其实有时候她是在远方
在天光和云影里
在花瓣和青草的汁液里
歌唱

百灵子其实就在我们中间

在我们激起轻浮之物的地方
她傲慢而美丽的面孔高高在上
所经之地　事物一律领受着光

香气汹涌如潮
鸟兽屏声敛息

百灵子　我红口白牙的姐姐
她背对着红尘歌唱
她在红尘之中歌唱

她用她歌唱的爪子
紧攥着　我下沉的心
和下沉的世界

百灵子在歌唱

Mary is Living in the World

My fiancée, Mary, is living in the world.

Mary, I'm your simple-hearted petty hunter.
I'll purchase ten thousand gardens
And put them to your charge.

Mary, believe it or not!

I swear by Astronaut Chuchettov[1] :
I'll, from the sky, the watery blue paper,
Scissor over half a slice of the moon, the golden yellow in
My heart, seemingly tiger colored,
As ornament to grace your gardens and your
Fair-complexioned and slender neck.

My fiancée, Mary
Please revel in your living in the world.

My ears are expecting you.
My greedy ears are still itching to hear your whispers,
Whispers with enchanting aroma—

My petty hunter, gray wolf.

How come you are still yourself?

When feeling lonesome, show your teeth

Glinting like a sword.

Let me treat you gentle.

My fiancée, Mary, a baker's daughter, is

Well steeped in the laws for dough fermentation.

Once in her presence, I turn soft and supple.

My fiancée, Mary, is living in the world.

My sweetie, my pure-hearted bonnie,

I insist she live in the world.

玛丽活在世上

我的女友玛丽活在世上

玛丽，我是你心地纯朴的小猎人
我要买下一万座花园
交由你来看管

玛丽，信不信由你

宇航员丘切托夫做证：
我要在天空　那水淋淋的蓝纸上
剪下半瓣还多的月亮　我内心的金黄
一种类似老虎的颜色
装饰你的花园　你的
又白又细的颈项

我的女友玛丽
你要好好地活在世上

我的耳朵在等着你
我的贪婪的耳朵还要听你的悄悄话
带着妖冶香味的悄悄话——

我的小猎人，大灰狼
你怎么还是你：
寂寞的时候　龇牙外露
剑的光芒
让我来给你温柔

我的女友玛丽　面包师的女儿
深谙制作发面的原理
她一出现　我就又绵又软

我的女友玛丽活在世上
心爱的人，心地单纯的人
我要她活在世上

The Bathing Maiden

Early morning, at three o'clock,

Water splashing sounds arise,

Her pure, greasy and aromatic body,

A glaring beam of white gleam.

Water around hopping and leaping,

Purely white, freshly bright,

Stirring up plumes of misty fog.

With her back to us,

In the dark, keeping distance

From the world, early morning at three o'clock.

Alone in the fountain, and in the fountain

She herself responds with bathing gestures and postures

In natural and slightly hesitant rhythms,

Water-flowering sounds

Penetrating the heart and lungs.

The maiden is bathing,

As if not bathing her body

Rather bathing a swan's

Neck inclining towards somewhere.

I dare say, the bathing maiden
She comprehends the darkness and the world.
And her choice of bathing at three o'clock early morning
Means she has a keener perception of beauty
And of the way to keep beauty in time and direction.

沐浴的少女

凌晨三时
水声响起
她净腻而芳香的身体
一道耀眼的白光
四周的水跳跃起来
洁白，鲜亮
激起阵阵迷蒙的雾

背对着我们
与世界保持着
凌晨三时的黑暗和距离

独自承受着泉　和泉中
一个人响应沐浴的各种姿势
自然而略含犹豫的律动
水开花的声音
穿透肺腑

沐浴的少女
仿佛不是沐浴自己的身体
而是沐浴一只天鹅

的不知探向何处的颈项

我敢肯定　沐浴的少女
她了解黑暗　世界
而选择在凌晨三时沐浴
则是她更了解美
美在时间和方向上保存的方式

Big Bronze Kettle

From lips to language, from long manicured fingernails

To headwear for shading,

A slim-waisted woman carrying

A slim-waisted big bronze kettle

Comes along with a gust of subtle bronze-glossed breeze.

The slim-waisted bronze kettle's big stomach has a big capacity.

It used to hold grains, salt, and a fish pregnant before marriage,

It also used to hold soils of deities ploughed by worms,

Yellow soils, black soils

And soils tasting no much flavor.

Emphasized by the big bronze kettle's big stomach,

Oh, how slim the slim-waisted woman is!

Inclusive of her slim legs, slender arms, fair-skinned neck

And implicitly elastic and delicate womb,

And slim forceful eyes more transparent than clear water.

The slim waist woman carrying a slim waist big bronze kettle

Comes up bringing a whiff of breeze more subtle than soul,

Bringing a cool and deadly fountain that

Only the big bronze kettle's big stomach can hold

And a gluttonous man desires to drink from but dares not to.

大铜壶

从嘴唇到语言　从修长的指甲
到头上遮阳的披饰
细腰女人抱着细腰的大铜壶
和一阵泛着青铜光泽的
细微的风走来了

细腰铜壶的大肚子大肚能容
曾装过粮食、盐和一条未婚先孕的鱼
也装过被蚯蚓犁过的属于神灵的土
黄的土、黑的土
和吃不出多少腥味的土

被大铜壶的大肚子强调着的
细腰女人的细呵
还包括她的细腿、长胳膊、白脖子
具有隐秘弹性的巧妙的子宫
和比清水还要明亮的细而有力的目光

细腰女人抱来了细腰的大铜壶
带来了一阵被灵魂还要细微的轻风
和只有大铜壶的大肚子才可容纳的

一个嘴馋的人想喝但又不敢喝的

清凉而致命的泉

A Contract with the Wolf-god

The simple coarse forest can no longer hold you.

No longer skim your gray silhouettes across hill-lips.

In the iron cage, you are no longer what you are.

Never can you be seen on the boundless northern steppe.

Ah, wolf-god—

(A contract with the wolf-god:

Sometime we'll fetch you home,

Open the yard gate, slaughter pigs and sheep

As if receiving our child back from exile.)

The world has changed, people raise everything.

Landlords and rich peasants raise snakes and scorpions,

But do not raise you.

Well-to-do men in cities raise pet dogs and lady-kins,

But do not raise you.

Ah, wolf-god—

(A contract with the wolf-god:

The city we live in is trapped deep in white,

Like death, a kind of white armed to teeth.

Window curtains, bed curtains, walls, ever-bright lights…
Oh, the inescapable white! We do not like it.

We need colors of other kinds, gray included,
The combative gray of yours when running.)

The world has changed. The darkness you need
Is being pined for by people as if reminiscing about a lamplight.
In the silver-white moonlight
Was nightingales' singing, an old wolf's sobbing
And a serene and nostalgic residence.
Ah, wolf-god—

We made a deal with our children: Allow you back!
Allow you not to just appear on television screens!

You are still yourself
Should stay on hillsides and fields, sneak-attacking and killing.
Should in the day idle on the street with an affectation of leisure,
See museums, exhibits of ancient weapons and hunting guns.
Should allow you, after occasional wrong-doing,
To titter without restraint,
To scare away someone's well-fed lady-kin.

Ah, wolf-god! We sign a contract with you —
Allow your gray to converge with the white of the herd,

Converge with the brownish red of the horses,

Converge with oceans, mountain forests, the skies—

The blue in our hearts.

与狼神签约

简单粗劣的林子不再容你
山唇之间不再飞掠你苍灰的剪影
铁笼中　你已不再是你
北方茫茫的草原上见不到你
狼神呵——

（与狼神签约：
什么时候我们接你回来
打开庭院，杀猪宰羊
就像接回自己流亡异乡的孩子）

世道变了，人们什么都养
地主富农养蛇养蝎但不养你
城里的阔佬养宠物狗小女人但不养你
狼神呵——

（与狼神签约：
我们所在的城市已深陷于白
像死亡，一种武装到牙齿的白
窗帘　床帐　墙壁　不夜灯
无处可逃的白呵我们不喜欢

我们需要另外的颜色　包括灰色
你在奔跑中杀气冲冲的灰色)

世道变了　你所需要的黑暗
像怀念灯一样正被人们怀念
白净的月色下
夜莺的歌唱和一匹老狼的哭泣
安静而怀乡的居所
狼神呵——

我们跟孩子们约定：让你回来
让你不仅仅在电视屏幕中出现

你还是你
应该在山坡上和原野里偷袭　杀生
白天还装模作样上街悠闲
参观博物馆和古代兵器陈列室
和各种猎枪　应该让你做完偶尔的坏事之后
情不自禁地窃笑
吓吓谁家饱食终日的小妇人

狼神呵，我们与你签约——
让你的灰色和羊群的白色汇合
和马群的棕红色汇合
和大海、山林、天空——我们心中
的蓝色汇合

The City of Toys

I'm a child of the old times. At a window of a deserted castle,

I'll recount a story that makes you thirstily parched—

Iron-like outstanding wolf packs,

A buck-toothed moon,

Firebirds stealing away the dark forest patch by patch,

The prairie and her poppy-like gaily colored stallions.

I am also a child of your times, but

As to this age, I find myself unable to leisurely narrate—

From iron to iron (*underground, above ground, and in the air*)

From city to city

From the first story, second...up to the hundredth of the building.

A maze of mirrors and maze-like mirrors

A mirror image. The children's faces are half given by parents

And half made of glass and another substance like that.

I am a child of your times, fear-stricken,

Anxiety-ridden, shuttling in the mirror-imaged labyrinth,

Without home, without direction.

I am a child of dream. Mine

Is a dream of Hercules[2]. The world

Is the city of toys in my dream, light as a feather—

The shadows of one thousand castles of imperial emperors are

Painted white by me.

Iron, in the way of tree roots,

Not only under body but under the whole city, is wriggling.

Such humidity of excessive humiliation and indignation!

Such humidity of the snake entangling the hare!

It's in gardens that mirrors are planted to exponentially

Magnifying the light to reflect into the snare of foxes and

Into the snare where the deer's

Heart has not yet stopped pulsating.

I am a child of dream.

I am a child of the world.

I reside in my city of toys.

玩具城

我是旧时代的孩子　在废弃的城堡的窗口
我要讲出令你口渴难耐的故事——
铁一样出色的狼群
獠牙似的月亮
火鸟怎样一片一片偷走黑森林
草原和她罂粟般鲜艳的公马

我也是你们时代的孩子　但
关于这个时代，我无法从容讲述——
从铁到铁（地下、地上和空中）
从城到城
从大楼的一层、二层……一直到第一百层
镜子的迷宫　迷宫似的镜子
镜像。孩子们的脸一边是父母给的
一边是玻璃和另一种类似的材料做的

我是你们时代的孩子　疑惧
顾虑　穿梭于镜像的迷宫
没有家乡也没有方向

我是梦的孩子　我的梦

是大力士的梦　世界

是我梦中轻如鸿毛的玩具城——

一千座帝王城堡的阴影被我涂成白色

铁和树根是一样的

不仅在身体以下而且在整座城市以下　扭动

羞愤难当的湿度

蛇盘兔的湿度

镜子是花园里种出来的　把光亮

成倍成倍地放大

投射到狐狸的陷阱　和鹿的

心脏并未停止搏动的陷阱

我是梦的孩子

我是世界的孩子

我居住在我的玩具城里

Notes:

[1] Chuchettov（丘切托夫）：Chuchettov is a name coined by the poet to refer to an astronaut in imagination.

But the first astronauts on the moon in real history are Neil Armstrong（尼尔·阿姆斯特朗）, Buzz Aldrin（巴兹·奥尔德林）, and Michael Collins（迈克尔·柯林斯）：

On July 20, 1969, half a billion people （a sixth of the world's population at the time） in 49 countries watched a ghostly black-and-white television image as Neil Armstrong backed down the ladder of the lunar landing ship Eagle（阿波罗 11 号的鹰号登月舱）, planted his left foot on the moon's surface, and said, "That's one small step for a man, one giant leap for mankind." （"这是个人的一小步，却是人类的一大步。"）

Twenty minutes later, his crewmate, Buzz Aldrin, joined him, and the world watched as the men spent the next two hours bounding around in the moon's light gravity, taking rock samples, setting up experiments, and taking now-iconic photographs. The third member of their crew, Michael Collins, orbited overhead in the Apollo 11 command ship, Columbia.

The first human being to travel into space is Soviet cosmonaut Yuri Alekseyevich Gagarin（尤里·阿列克谢耶维奇·加加林）. Yuri Alekseyevich Gagarin （9 March 1934 – 27 March 1968） was a Soviet pilot and cosmonaut. He was the first human to journey into outer space, when his Vostok spacecraft completed an orbit of the Earth on 12 April 1961.

[2] Hercules （赫拉克勒斯大力神）：Hercules is a huge muscular figure, usually shown bearded, sometimes not, wearing the skin of the Nemean lion（尼米亚狮子）, and carrying either a club or a bow and arrows. He is probably the most well-known of all the Greco-Roman gods （希腊罗马神）. Hercules was born a demigod with physical strength surpassing even that of the gods. The greatest and mightiest hero of ancient Greece, Hercules' name is synonymous with strength.

Part Five　Absolute High Landscape

Pilgrimage to Terra-cotta Army[1] Array

I'm standing here,

Standing here,

As though for thousands of years

Bronze, horses and my ancestors

All the time standing in deep-layers of the earth.

No longer does anything exist at all.

The sunlight, like Hukou Waterfalls[2],

Pours down from the legendary sky.

Something more profound than sunlight

Roars like a loud thunderbolt overhead.

The sunlight inspires me to rise breaking the sky.

Then, something more profound than sunlight

Forbids me to go back to the legend and the sky.

Something more profound than sunlight

Forces me, in a split second, to become a power bomb

To aim at the terracotta army array, dropping down,

To aim at the wilds of ages exposed again to the daylight,

To aim at bronze and my ancestors, dropping bombs frenziedly.

Beyond something more profound than sunlight,

Who is it that made them burst out crying

And made them suddenly run off in all directions,

Run to every single living human being, and strip off bronze

As if running to their kinsfolk in the rear zone and

Flinging themselves into the arms of their kinsfolk, wailing

More profound than the sunlight, and strip off bronze,

Recounting more profound than wailing?

谒兵马俑军阵

我站在这里
站在这里
就像几千年来
青铜、马匹和我的祖宗
一直站在地层深处

什么都不复存在
阳光如同壶口瀑布
自传说的天空倾泻而下
比阳光更加深刻的东西
轰叫如雷击中头顶

阳光激励我破天而起
之后，比阳光更深刻的东西
拒绝我回到传说和天空
比阳光更深刻的东西
迫使我在瞬间变成重磅炸弹
照准这兵马阵倒跌下来
照准重见天日的千古荒原
照准青铜与我的祖先狂轰滥炸

比阳光更深刻的东西之外

是谁使他们突然哭叫起来

使他们突然四散奔跑

奔向每一个活人　揭去青铜

如同奔向后方的亲人

使他们扑入亲人的怀抱

比阳光更深刻地痛苦　揭去青铜

比痛苦更深刻地诉说

Absolute High Landscape

1

Absolute great landscape was born

Half a century ago,

The endless earth was brilliant as fire,

On the earth, a life

More majestic than water,

A man named Mao Zedong was walking in Shanbei[3],

Like a fire dragon walking amid the flame.

When a nation sunken in tribulations,

He was walking through the flame for it,

For it he enjoyed the serenity in the flame.

2

One early morning, 1936[4],

The northern landscape and Mao Zedong stood together,

Looking up at the white clouds of Genghis Khan[5],

At Tang and Song Dynasties rise and fall into ruins and weeds,

At piles and piles of snow fading into mountains

And at rubbles and debris,

Mao Zedong was imbued with

A flame-like pure mood—

At last I understand these seasons,

The seasons that in the still time

Retrogress with a crash like thunder.

If in winter, if I were wind,

I'd hold breath in concentration,

Like snow-capped mountains, like ice-frozen rivers.

If in spring, if I were water,

I'd stay deep together with the huge river

To greet the coming of a deluge.

3

Oh! The unprecedented landscape of the loess plateau[6]!

Fighting chunks and chunks of spraying iron in the fire,

Under the rains and winds of ribs flying around

Safe and sound,

The realm of the flame center was getting higher and higher—

At last I'm bitterly aware of wind and water.

At last I'm aware

I belong to the wind and also belong to the water,

I'm in the wind and also in the water.

In the water, I'll be a human-faced fish,

All bitter expressions buried deep down the water.

In the wind, I'll be a giant fish beyond the water surface

By the name of Kun[7], furiously pecking the vault of heaven.

At last I understand my beloved people.

I'm familiar with them, I must

Walk along with them.

Oh my beloved people!

Oh wind! Oh water!

The water flows and flows,

Then will suddenly accumulate into a ferocious deluge.

All the hullabaloo will be silenced in the water,

The only water.

The wind blows and blows,

Then will shake the sky and the earth

For the returning of water, eternal wind!

4

Thus is the absolute great landscape,

Rooted in fair winds and pure water,

And with serenity in the fire

Beyond water and wind,

Getting close to sunshine, getting crowds who are apt at farming,

Adjacent to vast stretches of grains

Stretching ahead of them,

To appear appealing and to approach the dream.

No matter how congested the buildings will be

And how they will further thrive,

No matter how reinforced concrete mixes with plastic,

In the wind, our feelings akin to water and fire

Will never die off in tens and thousands of years to come.

Tens and thousands of things will never outgrow

The heavenly incomparable height of the flame.

绝对高度上的风景

一

绝对伟大的风景诞生于
半个世纪前
无边的土地辉煌如火
土地之上，一个比水
更磅礴的生命
一个名叫毛泽东的人行走陕北
如卷火之龙行走于火焰的中心
在一个民族沉入苦难之后
他为它而穿越火焰
他为它而享受火焰中的宁静

二

这是一九三六年的清晨
北国风光和毛泽东一同伫立
抬头仰望成吉思汗的白云
仰望夷为废墟草莽的唐盛宋衰
那一堆堆依山远去的瑞雪
和残砖断瓦

毛泽东满怀

火焰般淳朴的心境——

我终于懂得了这些季节

这些在静静的时间中

轰然倒退的季节

如果是冬季如果我是风

我将凝神屏息

如群山之雪，长河之冰

如果是春季如果我是水

我将厮守大河深处

迎候洪水来临

三

黄土高原空前绝后的风景呵

反抗火中大块大块飞溅的钢铁

在肋骨四起的风雨之下

相安无事

火焰中心的境界越来越高——

我终于痛切地感到了风和水

终于感到

我属于风也属于水

我在风中我也在水中

在水中，我将是人面鱼

所有凄苦的表情都在水底深藏

在风中，我将是超越水面之鱼
其名为鲲，怒啄苍天

我终于懂得了我亲爱的人民
我熟悉他们，我必须
与他们同行
我亲爱的人民呵
风呵水呵
那水流着流着
就会腾变为暴戾的洪水
一切喧嚣都将寂静于水
唯一的水
那风吹着吹着
就会摇天撼地
为了水的回归，永恒的风

四

绝对伟大的风景就这样
根植于良好的风中纯净的水中
并以超越水和风之上的
火焰中的宁静
与阳光亲近，使工于农业的人群
紧靠着他们面前大片大片
展开的庄稼
美丽动人接近梦境

无论楼房怎样拥挤

并进一步生长

无论钢筋水泥和塑料怎样结合

风中，我们如水趋火的心情

万千岁月也无法泯灭

万千事物也长不过

火焰天堂般无与伦比的高度

The Oriental Home

In the oriental home,

Walls are no longer the most significant contents,

Still grasses finally bred birds chirping and flowers fragrant.

These days

The mutilated fingers of the aged faintly rise and fall,

The sunlight shines upon the nun-like ground,

Sunlight unusually solemn.

These days, door-knocking arises everywhere.

Even the walls are pushed open,

These walls can't be any higher,

These walls can't be any thicker,

These are the walls we've for years woven with care,

Ah, the oriental home!

Yet even the walls are also pushed open.

Through the huge fissures,

Hands are reached in,

Hair is blown in,

A certain breath never existed before

Is fighting with us for silence through squabbling.

These days, or these days after thousands of years

My father seeks the lost sheep and mistakenly enters the city,

And has aged into a dejected teenager.

O my pitiful father!

These days

He stays on the road on the outskirts, from where

The carts went away,

Gazing at the dusk, recollecting memories of the home.

东方家园

东方家园

墙已不是最重要的内容

宁静的草莽终于养育出鸟语花香

这些日子里

老人们残损的手指依稀起落

阳光照亮修女似的大地

阳光肃穆异常

这些日子里到处响着敲门声

连墙壁也给掀开了

这些墙壁高得不能再高

这些墙壁厚得不能再厚

这些墙壁多年来我们细心编织

东方家园呵

可是连这墙也给掀开了

巨大的裂缝里

手伸进来

头发飘进来

一种从未有过的气息

吵着和我们争夺沉默

这些日子里，几千年后的这些日子里

我的父亲寻找丢失的羊误入城市

老成一个忧郁的少年

可怜我的父亲

这些日子里

他守住郊外马车远去的路

望着暮色怀念故乡

The Last Folk Songs[8]

Along the north, I went up the river,

Flocks of flying birds faded into the sky day by day.

Over the water, I increasingly ascended myself,

Attempting to approach the last folk songs.

The last folk songs floated into the sky,

The last folk songs in the flocks

On the broken wings are blown away by gusting winds.

I had no boat but

The last shoes left. The winter approached in due time,

Like a sharp blade

Piercing my blood vessels and soul,

I called soundlessly, tears dampening the clothes.

Ah, the north!   At the classical heights

The last few folkniks are already beyond the end of land.

The last one girl with protruding eyebrows

Vanished into the deep of folk songs;

My valentine in memory bends as a bowstring

Sweeping the floors for the wealthy in the city behind me.

Mountain peaks towering,

Amongst mountain peaks there remains but one single tree.

Ah, the north! Like a doomed decline!

In this modern age,

Folk songs as far as the sky left me woeful,

I called soundlessly, tears dampening the clothes.

Yet the big river at my foot is howling,

Enkindling affection and indignation.

最后的民歌

沿着北方，我溯河而上
成群的飞鸟在天空日渐苍茫
在水之上，我不断地上升自己
企图亲近最后的民歌
最后的民歌飘上天际
最后的民歌在鸟群之中
在折断的翅翼之上被大风吹散

我没有船
最后的鞋子　如期而至的冬天
像犀利的刀锋
穿透血脉和灵魂
我无声地呼唤　泪湿衣襟

北方呵　在古典的高处
最后一些唱民歌的人已越出大地尽头
最后一个睫毛高耸的女子
自民歌的深处消失
我记忆中的情人弯曲如弦之身
在我身后的城市为富人扫地

群峰高耸

群峰之中唯一坚守的树木

北方呵　仿佛注定的衰落

在这个摩登的时代

远至天际的民歌使我哀伤

我无声地呼唤　泪湿衣襟

而我脚下的大河咆哮着

激起柔情和悲愤

Qinling

When the whole world becomes a heap of hairy desolation,
The Qinling Mountains still exists, the Qinling Mountains
Still remains faithful like a hairy god,
Majestically and leisurely waiting,
With its wanton heap-up of grass, trees, broken stalks and dales,
Waiting for the re-birth of next one humankind.

When Qinling Mountains becomes a heap of hairy desolation,
God still exists on the grassland at its summit.
When God were to create next one world,
It would definitely follow the example of Qinling,
Imitating the way the Qinling Mountains bears grass and trees
And the way it brings forth demons and monsters
To let the world itself naturally and accordingly
Grow out of the desolation.

秦岭

在全世界变成一堆毛茸茸的废墟的时候
秦岭还在　秦岭
依然充满信念　像一个毛茸茸的神一样
雍容而自在地等着
用它的草、树、断茎和幽谷无节制的堆积
等待下一个人类再一次诞生

当秦岭变成一堆毛茸茸的废墟的时候
神依然在它顶端的草地上
神在创造下一个世界的时候
一定是取法秦岭
模仿秦岭生草长树的样子
和生妖变怪的样子
让世界自自然然
从废墟上长出来

Fossils

In the north

Under the cloudless leaden sky

The impoverished mountains have silenced thousands' years,

I am silenced.

Ah! Plateau

Gradually got rugged and far-stretched in the maddening weight.

Ah! Plateau

Simply left me alone moving restlessly around the cottage and

Failing to tread a road out through the desolate grass.

And in those moments of glorious sunshine after rain

I would always bend perching on the crude threshold,

I would always, through spider-webs sprawling the eaves,

Bear the sunlight profoundly sliced by spider thread.

The inhumane silence has lingered on too long,

I can endure no more. Ah, plateau!

The somber journey is just ahead,

I'd desert the petty birthplace,

I'd, with yarrow [9] on shoulder, head off to a distant land.

Never stop me, never!

Please, for my lot after departure and for tomorrow's journey

Shed tears or chant prayers

Or scorn and curse

But never stop me!

I' m aware, profoundly aware that

Thunders would end up crashing my life.

Some day   some moment

Surging mountains and billowing valleys

Would rip me into pieces in revelry of the vast ocean.

In billions upon billions of years,

One archaeologist would, from the deep wasteland

Behind the ocean, dig out my fossil,

Narrowly eye this tormented solidification, then promptly

The universe would be enveloped in meditation and exploration.

When the hammer gently strikes the fossil,

In my costal bone will echo the whizzing throughout the ocean

—The unyielding turbulence of a life!

化石

北方
在铅灰色的晴空下
贫瘠的大山千百年地沉默着
我沉默着

高原呵
在疯狂的力量中渐趋不平和深远
高原呵
任凭我不停地在茅屋四周躁动
那荒凉草丛中总不能踏出一条道路
而当雨过天晴、艳阳高照的那些时刻
我总是要委屈在简陋的门槛上
总是要透过遮掩整个屋檐的蛛网
承受被蛛丝深深割伤的阳光

残忍的沉默延续得太久了
我已不能忍受，高原呵
阴暗的旅程就在眼前
我要离开委琐的故乡
我要背负著草远奔异国他方
不要挽留我，不要

为了我走后的命运和明天的路程

流泪或者祈祷

或者鄙弃和诅咒吧

但是不要挽留我

我知道，深深地预料

雷电最终会把我的生活击毁

总有那么一天，那么一个时刻

澎湃的浪山涛谷

会将我撕裂成苍茫大海狂欢的碎块

而亿万年后

一个考古学家，会在大海之后

在荒原深处掘出我的化石

仔细端详着这个痛苦的凝固

天地间顿时充满沉思和追索

当榔头轻轻敲击化石

我的肋骨里会响彻大海的呼啸

—— 一个生命永不屈服的动荡

Behind a Red Cloth is White

Behind a red cloth is white,

Behind white is blue—

Somewhat lost inane blue.

If the white behind a red cloth

Is the white of a lover's face,

Behind white is a thicket of reckless tree shades

Inexplicitly revealing

The roots' direction

If a red cloth makes me faint,

O red outshining that of a celebration, then merely use insipid

Fruits and wares to embellish

The shade, the birth, the ambiguous gaiety and grief. I dare say

The white of the world is worthy of it, a red cloth

Is more capable than a warbling bird

Of eulogizing common folks

Of eulogizing the indiscriminately enthusiastic life.

Facing the world's gloom,

The spotlessly clean season that can mirror cloud shadows,

Acute pangs, roads leading to the end of the land,

All these simple and plain beauty,

All these scenes clarified by the chime of the soul,

O a red cloth is so incredibly red!

I mean when facing a red cloth, red and white in sharp contrast,

The sky's blue above it or the black of black cloth,

Why do I still have to be so big-mouthed and long-tongued?

Refuse inanition, red and white are equally vehement.

一块红布背后是白

一块红布背后是白
白的背后是蓝——
若有所失的空虚的蓝

如果　一块红布背后的白
是那种亲爱的脸庞的白
白的背后是一丛冒冒失失的树荫
并不明了地陈述着
根的方向

如果一块红布使我晕眩
越过庆典的红呵　仅仅是用平淡
的果实和器物装饰
阴影，生育，暧昧的欢愉和悲伤　我敢说
世界的白是值得的，一块红布
比一声鸟鸣更有能力赞美苍生

赞美不分青红皂白热烈的生活

面对世界的阴郁
可以映现云影的一尘不染的季节

剧痛，通向大地尽头的道路
这些简单明了的美
这些为灵魂的钟声而澄明的场景
一块红布真红呵

就是说面对一块红布　红白分明
它之上天的湛蓝或黑布似的黑
我为什么还要多嘴多舌：

拒绝虚无，红与白同样强烈

Escape to the Moon

Escape to the moon,

Once begun, there's no ending.

A kind of conflagration rolled up cloudy smoke up the skies,

A kind of soil came from afar shaking the earth,

Some people came along the road

To bid me farewell.

As if doomed by fate,

I, dust-faced,

In the seas of people

Living through gales and storms.

I, dust-faced,

Lingering in the depths of sorrowful melodies.

Fits of cruel desperation resembling April grass scent

Attacked me sudden.

At last, I arrived on the platform

Yet left the dusk alone awaiting

The last train.

Just like trees in fall shedding leaves,

Escape to the moon!

In the dark,

In the foggy night,

In the pitter-patter of rain stands aloof the huge platform,

Memories rising and falling like leaves.

Oh! My distant mountains!

Once the flood of doomsday ceases, I'll start on my way.

Floods are marshaling in my artery,

Floods are howling deep inside of me

Rising and falling in the lofty old walls,

Floods break the walls through,

Flooding to places afar.

Oh! My distant mountains!

Miserably, journeys far, roads long.

Soul, like baggage with shoulder strap fretted broken,

Suddenly breaks loose,

Falls splattering into the water, drenching me.

Miserably, wife separated, son astray. Mother

Still stands on the bank seeing me off.

All the year round, she's been crying my infant name.

All the year round, she's been weeping and sobbing.

The city I went through time and again,

Where walking steps stand out like disorderly shadows,

Is lonesome tonight.

Escape to the moon,

Dog-tired, dog-tired!

Just lean against certain background,

Thinking, facing the skies perpetual and remote.

Lean against certain background,

Thinking, too profound and remote.

Then know

The last train has already been missed.

Then know

Escape to the moon,

Escape to the legendary beauty,

Once begun, there's no ending.

向月亮逃亡

向月亮逃亡
有始无终

一种火灾卷起漫天云烟
一种土自远方动地而来
一些人从大路上走来
为我饯行

仿佛命中注定
我满面尘灰
在茫茫人海
历尽大风和暴雨
满面尘灰
在悲怆的旋律深处周旋
残忍的绝望酷似四月草香
阵阵袭来
终于赶到站台
却只留黄昏在等
最末一次班车

如秋季的大树落英缤纷

向月亮逃亡

黑暗中

夜茫茫雾蒙蒙

雨响声里兀立巨大的站台

回忆之叶潮起潮落

我的远山呵

末日的洪水刚停息我就上路了

洪水归结到我的动脉里

洪水在我的深处啸叫

在高峻的老墙里起落

洪水破墙而出

冲着远方泛滥

我的远山呵

难言路途漫漫

灵魂，像磨断肩绳的包袱

蓦然脱落

溅入浸我之水

难言妻离子散，母亲

还站在送我的河畔上

终年累月喊我小名

终年累月嘤嘤哭泣

我一次次经历的城市

走人的台阶伸出杂乱的影子

今宵落寞

向月亮逃亡

很累很累

就靠在某种背景上

遥对永恒苍穹遐想

靠在某种背景上

过于悠远地遐想

就知道

最末一次班车已经误点

就知道

向月亮逃亡

向传说的美丽逃亡

有始无终

Ten Thousand Moons Are Falling for Me

Ten thousand moons are falling for me.

The last moon

Shines cold light on the ground

And tonight brightens me again.

Harboring in heart the munificence of a withered tree,

In the abstract time and wind,

I peer at the archaic bronze,

A kind of face profounder than soil,

A kind of expression older than fire

A kind of face ordinary,

Without facial expressions like floating dust.

People without facial expressions just like dust

Come expressionlessly like dust carrying me along,

Infiltrating me like in an electrified way,

To let the last moon

Along with the cold light on the ground brighten me.

A kind of face also extraordinary,

Like a secret classic.

A kind of face is the dispiritedness after intoxication,

Totally dejected with love-sick.

Alone, having just trodden the wilderness,

Alone, sitting on the stone,

My eyes laden with dismay.

Ten thousand moons are falling for me.

The last moon

Is the ever-lasting moon.

This is the last evening,

The archaic bronze is glistening.

Seeing no end,

Nor beginning.

Just like the progenitors of many years ago, old as dirt,

Just like tonight's moon and cold light brightening me,

Tonight I'm delicately eye-browed and eye-glistened.

Oh! The glistening archaic bronze in the moonlight!

The man is all along standing upright,

Monotonously standing like in a nightmare of night,

Monotonously watching like in a nightmare of night,

People are like in a nightmare solitarily flicking by.

Ten thousand moons are falling for me.

After me, after tonight

The last moon tonight will become the beginning,

The cold light on the ground tonight will become the ending.

The moon tonight is the everlasting moon.

一万个月亮为我而落

一万个月亮为我而落
最后一个月亮
照出大地上的寒光
在今夜又把我照亮

怀着病树的宽宏大量
在抽象的时间和风中
我注视古铜
一种脸型深远于土
一种神情苍老于火

一种脸型普普通通
飘荡的尘土一样不着表情
一如尘土般不着表情的人们
尘土般不着表情地卷我而来
触电般地渗透我
使最后一个月亮
连同大地上的寒光把我照亮

一种脸型也不平常
像一部秘传的经典

一种脸型是大醉后的颓废

苦恋的黯然神伤

一个人刚刚走过荒原

一个人坐在石头上

满目怅惘

一万个月亮为我而落

最后一个月亮

是万古的月亮

这是最后的夜晚

古铜闪闪发光

看不到结局

也看不到开始

一如许多年前的先人苍老如土

一如今夜的月亮和寒光将我照亮

今夜的我眉清目秀

月亮下放光的古铜呵

那个人始终站着

噩梦般单调地站着

噩梦般单调地看着

众人噩梦般踽踽而过

一万个月亮为我而落

在我之后，在今夜之后

今夜的最后一个月亮将成为开始
今夜大地上的寒光将成为结局
今夜的月亮是万古的月亮

Worship

In the north, I see

Father walking afar toward the depths of the ground.

After father's departure,

Some peasants beyond the sound of water

Keep murmuring to the stone.

I see mother repeatedly scrabbling salt grains off the huge stone

And putting them into her thirsty mouth.

I see some other places that have a temple,

Some places that used to have a temple.

The stones, like lofty huge houses and ruins,

Put more people kneeling a long time, praying

Before father's departure,

Before father's father's departure.

Dusty and bloody heads are born in summer,

Suffering continual knocking and bumping from dawn to dusk,

This is the fate of the ground.

Then the sunlight brightens the upright-standing yellow soils,

Then the sun-brightened yellow soils fall from high

To give the silent village

And the people praying in silence

A hard-to-describe blow.

In the north, I also see

In the days long after father's departure

People refuse to shed blood and sweat to death

Yet don't familiarize with starting wars, O people!

O people, like stones, well adept at settling down for life!

They sit idle beyond the sound of water,

Far beyond the water in close observation.

Mother again takes charge of the yard

As if an auspicious moment will befall.

崇拜

在北方，我看见
父亲向着大地深处远走高飞
父亲走后
一些农人在水声之外
对着石头低语不休
我看见母亲从巨石上反复刮起盐粒
填入饥渴的口中

我看见另外一些有庙宇的地方
一些曾经有庙宇的地方
石头以大屋和废墟的巍峨
使更多的人长跪不起　　祈祷
父亲未去之时
父亲的父亲未去之时

蒙灰蒙血的头颅在夏天诞生
从早到晚不断遭受磕碰
这是大地的命运
于是阳光照白了站直身子的黄土
于是阳光照白的黄土自高处落下
给沉默的村庄

给沉默中祈祷的人群

以无法言喻的打击

在北方我还看见

我父亲走后很久的日子

众人拒绝流尽血汗而亡

却不熟悉发动战争，众人啊

石头般善于安身立命的众人啊

他们在水声之外枯坐

在隔水的远处密切关注

母亲重新操纵院落

仿佛吉祥的一刻将要降临

Notes:

[1] Terra-cotta Army（兵 马 俑）: The terra-cotta army, as it is known, is part of an elaborate mausoleum created to accompany the first emperor of China, Emperor Qin Shi Huang（秦始皇）, founder of the Qin dynasty（秦朝）, into the afterlife and guard his final resting place, according to archaeologists. The life-size warrior figures included chariots, weapons and horses, and were sculpted in impressive detail, down to their hairstyles and the insignias on their armor. Terra-cotta Army or Army of Terra Cotta Warriors are on display in the Museum of Qin Terra-cotta Warriors and Horses（秦始皇兵马俑博物馆）, which is located about 50kilometers east of the Xi'an City. Xi'an, once the capital city of 13 dynasties with a history of over 2,000 years in China, also got the fame as the eastern terminus of the Silk Road（丝绸之路）, where camels came and went for carrying kinds of goods and bridged the gap between the East and West.

[2] Hukou Waterfalls（壶口瀑布）: Hukou Waterfalls is in the middle reaches of the Yellow River and is the only yellow waterfalls on earth as well as the second largest in China after the Huangguoshu Waterfalls（黄果树瀑布）in Guizhou（贵州）. It is located in Yichuan County（宜川）in Yan'an City（延安）, Shaanxi（陕西）, China.
When the Yellow River flows to the place, the water of the river is squeezed by mountains on both banks into a narrow gorge like the spout of pot, and rushes rapidly and in the end cascades dramatically into a stone pond below, forming an illusion of water being poured with a height of 20 meters from a kettle, hence its name "Hukou or Kettle spout". Like thousands of tumbling dragons or enraged animals that have just been set free, the mountains echo with the deafening sound of the roaring water plunging down and pounding against the stones, which could be heard several kilometers away. During the rainy season, the waterfall's width stretches to a staggering 50 metres although on average, it has a width of 30 metres. The most dramatic changes occur during deep

winter and early spring when the river surface becomes frozen. Sometimes, the subsidiary falls freeze into icicles, creating images of crouching beast on top of the cliffs.

【3】 Shanbei （Northern Shaanxi 陕北）: Shaanxi, literally means "Land west of Shan" is a province located at the Northwest China region. Shan was the ancient name of the narrow mountain pass where the Yellow River flows from the Loess Plateau down to the North China Plain （华北平原）. Shaanxi borders the autonomous region of Inner Mongolia to the north and also borders Shanxi, Henan, Hubei, Sichuan and Gansu Provinces. Shaanxi region has bred 10 feudal dynasties, including Xia, Zhou, Qin, Han, Sui and Tang（夏、周、秦、汉、隋、唐）. Its current capital city, Xi'an （Chang'an in ancient China）, is one of the four great ancient capitals of China and the eastern terminus of the Silk Road.

Shanbei is an important frontier stronghold in ancient times, leaving historical relics such as Zhenbeitai （镇北台） of the Great Wall in Yulin （榆林）. It is the foothold of CPC Central Committee （中共中央） and the Central Red Army's Long March （中央红军长征）, as well as the starting point of the Eighth Route Army's （八路军） rush to the frontline of resistance against Japanese aggression. In Shanbei, Yan'an city is the place where the CPC Central Committee have fought and lived for 13 years. Yan'an spirit, cultivated by the old-generation revolutionists and communists is our Party's precious spiritual wealth. "Time and time again back to Yan'an in my dreams, I put my arms around Mount Baota." More and more people are coming here to receive education of the Party's fine traditions and working style for strengthening the spiritual power to remain unchanged to our initial motivation for the mission we will complete.

【4】 1936: The year 1936 witnessed a great event in Chinese history. In 1936, in order to support and respond to the Anti- Japanese and National salvation movement to push forward the establishment of Anti-Japanese and National united front, the Chinese Communist Party started the eastern expedition of Red Army （红军东征） as the first important strategic step.

On 26th of 1936, Mao Zedong and Peng Dehuai （彭德怀） led the Red Army's Long March troops （红军的长征部队） to cross the Yellow River to get to the front line in Shanxi province （山西） fighting Japanese troops. In early

February, before crossing the river, Mao Zedong stopped at a village called Yuanjiagou（袁家沟）in Qingjian County（清涧）of northern Shaanxi.

On February 7th, Mao Zedong climbed onto the loess plateau for the inspection of the terrain, and was tremendously amazed by the grand northern landscape with snow profusely falling, blotting out the sky and the earth. Having marveled at the geographic high landscape of nature, Mao Zedong suddenly had a spiritual high landscape of lofty aspirations sprouting in heart and depicted it into a ci poetry named Qinyuanchun • Xue or The Spring Refreshing the Garden•Snow（《沁园春•雪》）, which turned out to be an outstanding lyric of snow in the field of Chinese poetry as well as his greatest poetic masterpiece:

What lofty northern landscapes!
What rivers in frozen shapes!
What immense snowing celestial drapes!
Lo! within the Great wall and far beyond,
All is covered with flying snow alone.
Upon the mighty river up and down,
Waters run still without flowing sound.
Mountains turn silver snakes swaying in wave,
Highlands turn wax elephants galloping in the white,
Vying with the sky dome for the supreme pride.
Wait till the day of glorious sunlight,
Wow, dressed in crimson, groomed in white,
What an exceptionally enthralling sight!
A vast land replete with such charm and beauty,
Numerous heroes so obediently bow with awe and piety.
What a pity! The emperors Qin Huang and Han Wu
Showed inferiority in cultural creativity;
The emperors of Tang Zong and Song Zu
Showed deficiency in their literary productivity.
And Genghis Khan, a heavenly pride at his time
Only versed in bending bows at vultures in the sky.
Forever is all gone,
For truly heroic figures, we can count on this age alone.

(Translated by Wen Shilong)

[5] Genghis Khan（成吉思汗）: Genghis Khan, "Khan of Khans（可汗之汗）", whose original name was Temujin（铁木真）, was in his day the supreme ruler of the Mongolian tribes. A great strategist and statesman, Genghis Khan was regarded by the Mongols（蒙古人）as a divine ruler. At the end of 12th century, he united Mongolian tribes and challenged other powers to expand his huge Mongolian empire, which extended from South China to the Caspian Sea（里海）.

In 1277, Khan attacked the West Xia Kingdom［西夏王国（presently Ningxia 今宁夏）］and encountered strong resistance. He died of disease and age. The great emperor was later buried secretly according to Mongolian custom. It says that after the burial, 2,000 men were slaughtered by some 800 soldiers who were in turn executed so that the location of the real tomb remains a secret.

Genghis Khan's Mausoleum（成吉思汗陵）, rebuilt in 1954, 185 kilometers south of Baotou（包头）, is a mausoleum, in which only his clothing is buried in memory of the great leader. The 5.5 hectares mausoleum includes three giant yurt halls which house coffins of the Khan, his wife, his son and his generals.

There are four sacrifice ceremonies held annually to commemorate the great hero and leader of the Mongolian people. The ceremony, held on March 21st on lunar calendar, is the grandest. After the ceremony, horse racing, archery and wrestling are held as entertainment.

[6] The loess plateau（黄土高原）: The loess plateau is located in the northwestern region of China, stretching across six provinces（Qinghai, Gansu, Ningxia, Shaanxi, Shanxi and Henan）and covering an area of 530,000 square kilometers. It is the largest loess plateau in the world. During the Palaeozoic Era（古生代时期）it was filled with a boundless ocean. During the later Palaeozoic Era it started to rise out of the water and transform into a magnificent subtropical landscape. In the Quaternary Period（第四纪）the strong northwestern wind began to transport dust and sand particles from Mongolia and Central Asia so that after millions of years of accumulation, the region became covered with loess and became a habitat for people to settle down. The loess plateau has an ideal environment for the development of cave dwellings, which are not only warm in winter but cool in summer, and very comfortable to live in.

【7】 Kun（鲲）: Kun is an imaginary fish that was depicted by the Chinese ancient philosopher Chuang Tzu（庄子）in *A Happy Excursion*（《逍遥游》）: "There is a fish in the North Ocean, called the Kun; the Kun changes into a bird called the Peng."（"北冥有鱼，其名为鲲，化而为鸟，其名为鹏。"）Peng, similar to roc, is a gigantic bird popular in ancient Chinese literature.

【8】 Folk songs（民歌）: Northern Shaanxi folk songs（Shanbei folk songs 陕北民歌）,whose original name is Xintianyou or roaming mountainous airs （信天游）, are an important artistic form in the area of Northern Shaanxi Province（陕北）. Northern Shaanxi folk songs are vivid reflections of local people's life and work. The folkniks（folk singers）there sing loud-pitched original folk songs to express their joys, angers, sorrows, pains, thoughts and so on so forth. The northern Shaanxi folk songs are not only beautiful in tune, but also contain rich folk culture of Northern Shaanxi, whose love songs are said to be paralleled to love songs in *the Book of Odes*（or *the Book of songs, the Book of poetry* 《诗经》）of ancient China in terms of aesthetic value.

【9】 Yarrow（蓍草）: Yarrow has a spicy floral scent that is useful to stimulate regeneration and heal skin ailments. Meanwhile, yarrow was employed for divination（占卜）in ancient times in China in predicting one's future fate tendencies.

第六辑　巫颂

Part Six　Ode to Wizardry

Legend

Open the face of the clouds,

Open the ridge leading to the dense fog and the horizon,

Twelve sheep and nine oxen follow me into the city.

Open the height of a big building,

In the utmost depths of stones and bricks,

Find the robbed horse and the pottery clay. At dusk,

A horse runs through the wall,

Galloping about in farther places.

The twelve sheep are head-dressed in silverware,

The nine oxen are clad in red silk.

Twelve sheep and nine oxen! What a solemn ceremony!

Twelve sheep and nine oxen are strengthening my procession.

Open the face of the city wall,

Open a jar of aged liquor buried under the city moat.

The hero in the liquor raises a machete,

He's the robber who looted my oxen and sheep.

Open the face of the liquor,

I am also the hero in the liquor. I see

Behind another building

Twelve sheep fall to their knees in prayer,

Nine straps of red silk and some blood stains

Rise with brilliant rays into the higher heavens.

Open the face of a horse,

I see the last few noble souls.   Farther away

Another horse hints to me to abandon the city and flee.

传说

打开云朵的面孔
打开通向浓雾与地平的谷背
十二只母羊和九头公牛随我入城

打开一座大楼的高度
在石头和砖头的最深处
找到被劫的马匹与陶土　在向晚时刻
一匹马穿墙而过
在更远的地方驰骋

十二只母羊头饰银器
九头公牛身披红绸
十二只母羊和九头公牛　庄严的仪式
十二只母羊和九头公牛为我壮大行程

打开城墙的面孔
打开护城河下埋葬的一坛老酒
酒中的英雄高举大刀
他是抢走我牛羊的强盗

打开酒的面孔

我也是酒中的英雄　我看见

在另一座大楼的背后

十二只母羊跪着祈祷

九块红绸和一些血迹

随着光芒上升到更高的天空

打开一匹马的面孔

我看见最后一些高贵的灵魂　在更远处

另一匹马暗示我弃城而逃

Supplication

Shatter me,

Let mountains, rivers and the land absorb.

Only if in my heart

Stones no longer flip and roll,

At all times,

I remain placid and pacified.

In absolute seclusion,

Picking up the pen, I'd feel deeply moved

To write down the lives of the people.

Shatter me,

Let mountains, rivers and the land absorb.

Only if in the stones deep underground

I'm still alive, stubborn like water,

Filtered down with difficulty, I

Day and night

Rise again along the roots,

Making clusters of wild grass sprout out the impoverished land,

Making many trees in turn line up into the body of the sky,

The flesh and garment no longer torturing my soul,

Pains extinct.

祈祷

把我砸碎
让山河大地吸收

只要我的心里
大石不再飞滚
所有的时刻
我平静祥和
在离群索居之时
拿起笔便深受感动
写下众人的生活

把我砸碎
让山河大地吸收

只要地层深处的石头里
我仍然水一样顽固地活着
艰难地滤下去的我
朝朝暮暮
沿着根系又升上来
使簇簇野草生出很穷的大地
使许多树依次排入天空的身体

肉体和衣服不再虐待灵魂

痛苦绝迹

Mask

Let the body become more decayed than in history
To make starlight, the gale （*It blew off many masks*）
And the dashing deities pass through more easily.

Lung lobes and kidneys treasure up blood and stones.
Let the mirror shine in, let the light reflected by the mirror
Feel your face stripped off mask
And the unornamented head of a psychopath.

The ribs of this era are elusive.
Any one night, the unbridled insomnia, adultery,
Stealthy garbage dumping
And singing pervasive like hullabaloo

Are persecuting me. I'm not fit to live here,
This damned rampant city!
The day before I leave, I'll shout at it
Loudly—

"You all, I can't stand the odds and ends you love.
Now I need a mask!"

The day before I leave,

I'll wear a mask.

I'll coin terms pieced together by words as dirty, messy, shoddy

To shout out.

I'll shout out to

Let myself grow genuine.

面具

让身体变得比历史上还要腐败
使星光　大风（它掀翻了多少面具）
和狂奔的神明更容易通过

肺叶和肾珍藏着血、石块
让镜子照进去　让镜子里返回的光
摸摸你放弃了面具的脸
和精神病患者般不修边幅的头部

这时代的肋骨难以捉摸
这任何一个夜晚都不加控制的失眠、偷情
偷倒的垃圾
歌唱像吵嚷一般地普及

逼迫着我。我已经不适合在这里居住
这个横行霸道的城市
等离开前的那一天　我将冲着它
大声嚷嚷——

"你们，这被你们热爱的什物我已忍无可忍
现在我需要面具！"

等离开的那一天

我要佩戴好面具

我要把脏乱差的词语　东拼西凑

大声嚷嚷一通

大声嚷嚷

让自己变得真实起来

Direction

Direction is related to the decline of imagination,

Related to nearsightedness, blindness and covetousness.

But I am a man still believing in destiny.

Through my palm prints in

Utter disorder, like branches destined for ailments,

I keep directions.

I closely observe the things that point to the sun in the day

And point to the lamplight in the night,

And the scenes in which things with shadows

How gratefully live on or pass away.

When the foliage like plumage of an injured bird

Fall off one upon another,

When a pair of big hands able to carry a boulder,

Owing to their inability to feed the only son or daughter,

Owing to their humiliation for failures time after time,

Owing to their excessive roughness (*even disclosing a tendency*

toward transformation into some animal) ,

Don't know where to place

Now problems of direction become problems of reality,
Namely the problems of destiny.

But I still tend to believe direction
Is the place you head for in dreams
And determine to dwell in.

方向

方向与想象力下降有关
与近视眼、盲目和贪婪有关

但我仍然是相信命运的人
我通过我的掌纹
混乱不堪　像注定会生病的树枝
的掌纹掌握方向

我注意观察着白天指向太阳
和夜晚指向灯光的事物
和有阴影的事物
怎样感恩地活着或死去的情景

当树叶如受伤的鸟羽
纷纷坠落
当一双搬动巨石的大手
由于无法养活仅有的儿女
由于羞愧而一次次扑空
由于过分粗糙（甚至显出向某类动物变异的倾向性）
不知该往哪里放

这时方向问题成为现实问题
也是命运问题

但我仍然倾向于认为　方向
就是你在梦中走去
并决定居住的地方

Tower[1]

I can't foretell the life behind stones.

Secrets after all stay speechless

Till languages die out.

Who can convince the jostling people

Into descending the winding stairs back to the ground

To look up at

What the hell happened.

As for the eagle at rest, they

Have their wings left behind at precipitous heights.

People shouldn't have nothing at all, people

Should either ascend to more precipitous boundlessness

Or in the end make a declaration.

塔

我无法预言石头背后的生命
秘密终久不吭一声
直至语言泯灭

谁能说服拥挤的众人
走下旋梯复归大地
抬头仰望
发生了什么事情

至于歇脚的鹰
留下翅膀在险峻处
人不该一无所有　人
要么升入更险峻的苍茫
要么最后声明

Jade[2]

Up till now, jade is deep in the mountains

In Shanbei, where I reside.

When I fall into silence,

In places within sight but beyond reach,

People standing at low places gaze with penetrating expectation.

The sunshine and the roof tiles are high overhead.

Beyond sunshine, O jade

Floats in the center of the windstorm

Floats in the unclean muddy water!

When I see some unclean people, O jade

Often times falls into pieces prior to eave tiles.

And just like romantic love having hurt the heroes,

Jade is the only thing prone to the land and time.

Where jade falls down,

Down with it heroes fall.

Where the heroes fall down,

Monuments stand nearby, monuments

Therefore are ashamed and embarrassed to death.

Therefore, in many years' time,

When the monument builders are gone with wind,

Broken pieces of jade will be brightened again by sunshine,

In fact monuments are always repenting by themselves

Behind the rank grasses and verdant mosses,

My face will turn pallid again.

玉

至今玉在深山

在我安身立命的陕北

在我陷入沉默之后

在可望而不可即的地方

站在低处的众人望眼欲穿

阳光和屋瓦高高在上

阳光之外　玉呵

飘荡于风暴的中心

漂荡于不干净的泥水里

当我目睹一些不干净的人时　玉呵

常常先于瓦当而碎

而就像爱情伤害了英雄

玉是唯一趋向大地和时间的事物

玉倒下去的地方

英雄也随之倒下

英雄倒下去的地方

纪念碑近在咫尺　纪念碑

因此尴尬得无地自容

因此在许多年后

当树碑人也随云烟消散

玉的碎片被阳光再度照亮

纪念碑其实一直在兀自忏悔

在草莽和苍苔之后

我的面容将再度惨白

Ode to Wizardry

Living in Shanbei, I'm

Doomed to associate with the soils empowered by deities.

After a big wind blows by,

In the coarse interior of rocks,

I see a good many sensitive shadows fleeting by.

They are in wizard-like profound meditation

Wishing to break out of the rocks with a thundering sound.

The deity-empowered soils put me to peace

Until a knife floats about hugely like noble music,

The heavenly dome cracks like water,

Floats out like smoke, like fog

And merges into the blue sky in a wild stormy way

Until a sort of melody pushes mountains, rivers and the earth;

Over the deep grasses and debris,

Doors once again stand up to open and close freely.

In the downpour of rain,

In the brilliant sunlight,

The rusting marks fall off the walls,

Falling, layer by layer.

Like people coming up from the ends of agriculture,

Coming up from the ends of the porch,

Coming up from sleepless and dreamful nights,

The empowered soils put me to peace, standing facing the wall.

At the moment, in the name of boulders,

When wizards threateningly approach slowly from deep,

For the sake of the next moment's storm,

I won't utter a single word.

For the next moment, I'll hold fast to tranquility in the storm,

Watching dust, crows and some other things

From the surface of life gradually fly away from

Shanbei behind the wind.　At the moment,

I stand facing the wall in rapt silence like a wizard.

巫颂

身在陕北

就注定要和通神的土为伍

一阵大风过后

在岩石粗糙的内部

我看见众多敏感的影子闪过

他们以巫者的深刻沉思默想

欲与雷霆之音破石而出

通神的土使我趋于安静

直至有刀子势若高贵的音乐在游动

天堂般的穹顶如水破裂

如烟似雾往外飘散

并以狂飙的方式融入蓝天

直至一种旋律推动山河大地

草莽和废墟的深度上

门重又站起来自由闭合

在大雨倾盆中

在阳光灿烂中

墙上的锈斑失落

层层失落

像人一样从农业的尽头走来

从楼道的尽头走来

从失眠和多梦的夜晚走来

通神之土使我趋于安静并面壁而立

这时，以巨石的名义

当巫们自深处缓缓逼近

为下一刻的风暴

我不能开口说话

为下一刻在风暴中恪守宁静

目睹尘埃乌鸦和另外一些东西

自生活表层冉冉飞离

身在大风后的陕北　这时

我默穆如巫并面壁而立

Witch

Upon putting up paper-cuts on the windows, Shanbei

Recommences to open that antique bronze lock.

Delicate fair arms and the gloss of a key

Are the beauty of my lover, polished for thousands' years.

Tonight, setting out from the depth of bones,

It seeks the sunlight that shone at midday,

It seeks me that was lost in the wind

On the day when a broken dream faintly awakened.

Though kneaded tremendously by winds, rains and times,

Orientation continues unchanged in the lunar calendar,

Aged paper deeds stay together with shrines of god up till now.

When dust is once again cleared up,

Before your eyes are all pure gold cast treaties.

Living in the cave dwelling, you let out a surprising cry,

All at once, jewels shine and bloom their brilliance,

In a dreamy way, carrying along soils that generations rely on.

A big river walks up through heavy blows and strikes.

When taken a bird-eye view of windy moments from high,

Shanbei, the unexpected beauty

In a dreamy way occupies more elevations.

A big river, in a mode far more elevated than dreams,

Rises and falls dramatically together with a man.

A window is opened repeatedly like this

To make me turn back one thousand times, turn back

And then turn forward

And turn back again

Tearfully staring at the re-established home after the flood.

Those witch-like faces fresh like ice and fair like gem,

For whom are they indulged in holding their breath

In half light and half shade?

In biting autumn winds, Shanbei is covered

With fallen leaves, much like dead souls refusing Heaven,

For whom the keening together with father's singing

Spread far and wide time and time again in a dreamy mode?

女巫

贴罢窗花，陕北
再开始打那道古铜的锁
皙白的手臂和一把钥匙的亮度
是我的爱人磨砺千年的美丽
今夜，从骨头的深度出发
它寻找正午发生的阳光
寻找残梦依稀醒来之日
在风中失传的我

纵使风雨光阴百般揉搓
持久于农历中不变的方位
陈年旧纸的契据至今与神龛同在
当尘埃再一次被打扫干净
满目都是纯金铸就的条约
屈居窑洞，你惊喜地喊一声
顷刻之间珠光宝气灿然怒放
以梦的方式挟持祖祖辈辈赖衍之土

一条大河在深重打击中走来
居高临下俯瞰有风的时刻
陕北，这始料未及的美丽

以梦的方式占领过更多的高度
一条大河以比梦更高的方式
与一个男人共同大起大落

一扇窗户就这样一再打开
使我一千次地回过头，回过头
又把头转过来
然后再次回过头
含泪注视大水之后重设的家园

那些女巫似的面孔冰清玉洁
为了谁在半明半暗中沉溺于屏息
在犀利的秋风中，陕北
满地落叶酷似拒绝天国的亡灵
为了谁哭声伙同父亲的歌声
以梦的方式一次次声名远播

Temple[3]

Coming back in halting steps, I'm approaching Shanbei again,
Some piled-up plain stones are honed with the village's gloss.
On the loess plateau with highlands protruding step by step,
Looking beyond the miscellaneous grain crops standing upright,
I see a towering temple and the bell chimes
Once again have forefathers and me and a big river
Deeply penetrated,
And placed in the high-qualified sunlight for parching.

Standing against wind, the temple occupies all the newest heights
Yet has been forsaken many times for my sake.
For history in the shade considering a bunch of kids for long,
My father and mother, obedient to religious service,
Behind the boundless mountains and the eastern hedge,
Back to back, covered faces weeping.

It reminds me of some wealthy household's enclosure wall
That can sometimes be a temple standing aloof from people.
Some people enter with reverence,
More others are denied entrance.
On thundering and lightning days, by

Electricity's incomparable sharpness and dignified generosity,

The world throughout is together engraved by scriptures of fate.

Facing high walls one upon another,

I, standing against the wind,

With mud washed off the feet in rivers, tail after all the way,

Silently hearing the temple doors fade out in twilight.

Heartened by tiding,

I suddenly pose my lips in a gaping state,

But after all can not cry out the sound of water.

In Shanbei, the temple guides a whole day to settle down.

Apart from the temple, I stand against the wind,

It's the ritual chosen by ancestors.

When sheep and the shepherd swim by in the dark,

In a flash, I'm aware of the secret oracle.

I must once again leave without saying farewell

I must, in a more remote place,

Force the deep buried water to accumulate and resound louder.

庙

蹒跚归来　再一次与陕北逼近
一些堆砌朴素的石头磨出村庄的亮度
在高地逐级竖起的黄土坡上
错过立于不败之地的五谷杂粮
我看见很高的庙堂和钟声
把祖先和我和一条大河
再一次深深穿透
并放置于阳光的高风亮节中烘烤

迎风而立　庙占领了所有最新高度
为我已被多次遗弃
为历史在背阴处长久斟酌一群孩子
我父和我母屈居礼拜的仪仗
在苍茫了群山和东篱之后
背对背掩面而泣

想起一些富人的围墙
有时也会独立众人之外成为庙堂
一些人恭恭敬敬走进去
更多的人被拒之门外
响雷打闪的日子

以电的无比锋利和雍容大度

普天之下同被命运的铭文刻中

面对一出又一出的大墙

迎风而立的我

就河濯净裹足之泥一路尾随

静听庙门在暮色中渐趋暗淡

为潮意的鼓舞

我的双唇徒然摆放张开的状态

终究喊不出水声

在陕北　庙引导一天的日子安定下来

除庙而外我迎风而立

是先人们选定的仪式

当羊群和牧人在黑暗中游过

蓦然间我心领神会了秘而不宣的神谕

我必须再次不辞而别

我必须在更远的地方

迫使深藏之水愈加浩大而嘹亮

Incense[4]

Incense is the most resonant wail in the orient.

I guess at the primary moment, sitting in the candlelight,

Grandmother cut open whoever's skin,

Then a surging big river was flowing overwhelmingly,

Incense following behind.

Those who stood facing the incense scampered along the river

Wailing for help, I remember

Smoke kept rising and breaking into pieces in the ashen space.

I in front, those people behind

Together embraced the grace of forefathers.

The village, where firewood always touches the sky, is

The sole place that incense frequents. I remember

Father's weathered hands were stiff-boned, grossly protruding.

He had to, time and time again, open the ground to

Suckle from mother and from deep roots decaying down.

Never aspire to retreat from the burning sound of incense,

It is boundlessly sedate and balmy. Some day

I'll deeply feel unusual pains when walking together with water,

Waves surging sky-high. Some day,

Through the center of a floating log,

I'll, together with incense and with people's unfamiliar weeps,

Swim through deep waters,

Seek access into the inaccessible. Oh, incense

Is on the big river advancing bravely along with waves.

In the great wilderness, in the far vision arched by tomb wood,

Who will open the last family tree in the forefather's hands

And fumigate off the blank space awaiting my name to fill in?

香

香是东方最嘹亮的啼哭

我想最初一刻　端坐烛影之中

祖母割开谁的肌肤

就有一条汹涌的大河直逼而来

香随其后

那些面香而立之人在大河边际飞奔

悲怆的呼救，我记得

青烟不断向上和碎于空间之灰

我在前　那些人在后

共同承蒙祖先的恩泽

柴火永远摩接天空的村庄

香唯一的来去之地，我记得

父亲风干的手掌骨质坚硬大起大落

他必须一次次打开大地

吮吸母亲以及一些废入深远之根

决不可梦想逃离燃香之音

它无边无际的安详温暖　有朝一日

我将深感与水同行异常疼痛

大浪滔天　有朝一日
透过一根游木的中心
我与香与人陌生的哭泣游穿深水
在未及之处寻求抵达　香呵

在大河之上随波奋进
在大荒之中，　在墓木成拱的远景里
谁会打开先人手中最后的家谱
熏去等着我名字的空白

Notes:

【1】 Tower（塔）： Towers serve all sorts of purposes. Early towers generally have been thought to be built for defensive reasons（implying warfare）, religious services, observatory purposes, or as a means of telecommunication.

Towers always astound you when you notice their zeniths brushing the clouds. From a distance, you can see a tower peering over the cityscape or acting as a beacon of light. Towers have been built by man since prehistoric times, and even today when it comes to building one, engineers and architects are faced with tremendous challenges because of the sheer height-to-base ratio that they need to maintain.

There are many famous towers in the world, such as the Eiffel Tower（埃菲尔铁塔）, which stands in the Champ de Mars（战神广场）, a park near the River Seine in Paris（巴黎的塞纳河）, and the Leaning Tower of Pisa in Italy（意大利的比萨斜塔）, which is most lop-sided.

There are also many famous towers in China, among which is the Yellow Crane Tower（黄鹤楼）in Wuhan. Standing on Sheshan（Snake Hill 蛇山）, at the bank of Yangtze River（长江）in Wuhan, Hubei Province（湖北省武汉市）, the Yellow Crane Tower is considered one of the Four Great Towers of China. Tourists can obtain a fine view of the Yangtze River（长江） from the top of it. It has the appearance of an ancient tower but was built with modern materials and includes an elevator. Displays are presented at each level. It is not only an important scenic spot, but also a symbol of "piping times of peace" in people's minds. Scholars and poets（like Cui Hao 崔颢 and Li Bai 李白）in the past dynasties wrote hundreds of poems and scores of writing in praise of the magnificent Yellow Crane Tower.

The Yellow Crane Tower - by Cui Hao
The ancient immortal flew away astride the yellow crane,
Leaving the Yellow Crane Tower forlorn and alone.
Once gone and never back, so is the yellow crane,

White clouds of ages keep afloat in the empty welkin.
Trees of Hanyang Town are bathed in the sunshine,
Grasses on the Parrot Isle flourish so lush and fine.
Nostalgia for Homeland arises in heart at dusk time,
Plumes of mist on the river make me groan and pine.

(Translated by Wen Shilong)

【2】Jade（玉）：Jade is a bright pearl in the history of ancient oriental civilization. It is the witness and practitioner of the idea of unity between man and nature. It is engraved with long and heavy stamps of history. As the old Chinese saying goes, "Without being worked, jade cannot be shaped into a vessel"（玉不琢，不成器）, each piece of exquisite jade has been released by the craftsman's fine craftsmanship, which is the glory of jade since ancient times.

China is the kingdom of jade. Chinese jade and jade culture have gone through a long history of 8,000 years, beginning in the Neolithic Age（新石器时代）. Their history is earlier than the oriental cultural forms of ceramics, writing, painting, sculpture, architecture, silk, etc. In the Neolithic Age, jade was the messenger of communication between the heavens and the earth; In the Xia, Shang and Zhou dynasties（夏、商、周三代）, jade was integrated into the national ritual and music system; After the Qin and Han dynasties（秦汉时期）, jade became a symbol of self-cultivation. In various historical periods, although jade presents different characteristics and meanings of the times, it is closely linked with the main line of development of Chinese civilization and Chinese culture, and has become an important way to study the evolution of ancient Chinese civilization.

As early as the Neolithic Age, the ancestors of the Kunlun Mountains discovered Hetian jade（和田玉）and transported it between the East and West as a treasure and friendship medium, forming the "Jade Road" of the oldest Hetian jade transportation channel in China, that is, the predecessor of the Silk Road. Hetian jade, which bears 8,000 years of glorious jade culture history, is a treasure of the Chinese nation. It is known as the "National Jade". It is like a pearl, radiating splendid brilliance in Chinese history and culture, and is one of the important symbols of the Chinese nation's moral spirit.

【3】Temple（庙）：The temple is usually a place of worship consisting of an edifice for the worship of a deity. However, in China, temples are mostly an important part of China's Buddhist heritage and culture, apart from Buddhist grottoes, mountains, and religious sites like the Leshan Giant Buddha（乐山大佛）. There are a lot of famous temples in China with magnificent layouts and traditional Chinese architecture, such as Famen Temple（法门寺）, a Buddhist temple; The Temple of Heaven（天坛）, a Taoist temple in Beijing, the capital of China; and The Temple of Confucius（孔庙）.

【4】 Incense（香）: The word incense means "fragrant substance". Incense and fragrances have been a part of Chinese culture for thousands of years. Using incense is regarded as a form of philosophy that transcends social boundaries. It is intertwined with Dhyana and meditation（禅宗和冥想）.

Part Seven　The Sound of Bronze

Grass

Grass was standing in a precious style

After huge stones sank into the ground,
After the gone-out livestock returned disappointed,
After floods repeatedly washed away our homes,
After fires and knives were taken away.

Grass was standing in a precious style,
Fascinatingly standing
On the northern wasteland.
Looked from afar,
Behind the grass were the skins of my ancestors,
Were bronzes and deserts.

Oh! The treasured grass! The whole afternoon
It learned the postures of sunshine,
With its own flowers soundlessly blooming alone.
When floods brought disasters after ancients,
Oh! The grass, hugely similar to my lifetime,
Embraced bursting buds in places beyond people's sight,
Whispering at the top of a broken stalk,
Standing the whole afternoon un-swayed by winds.

草

草珍贵地站着

在大石沉入大地之后
在出去的牲口们失望而归后
在洪水反复洗劫了我们的家园
在火焰和刀具被带走之后

草珍贵地站着
迷人地站着
在北方的荒原上
远远望去
草的背后是我祖宗的人皮
是青铜和沙漠

那珍贵的草呵　整个下午
它学习阳光的姿势
与自身的花朵悄然独放
当大水在古人之后带来灾难
酷似我一生的草呵
在众人不见的地方拥戴花蕾
在一根断茎的顶端密语
整个下午不为大风所动

Horse

Well, you,

Born in the age when people no more go horse riding,

Are predestined to be solitary all life

Predestined to be a wild horse, running hither and thither,

Taking the grasslands for granted,

A wild horse without any aim,

Not able to stop running

Until too exhausted to keep on

A horse with talent but no virtue, a starving horse,

A horse fond of running, fond of slothfully

Lying at ease on the wild fields

A horse gazing at wild flowers,

Deadly exhausted,

Too exhausted to even intend to graze extra mouthfuls of grass.

Well, such a person you are, when you are aged,

When turned a horse with old age,

O forlornly-wretched and skinny-boned horse,

Still keep on

Still keep on running

Running without a stop.

You, a wild horse,

Are predestined to be a horse,

A destined horse.

马

你这个人
生在人已不再骑马的年代
命里注定要孤独一生

命里注定是一匹野马　到处跑
对草原不以为然
没有什么目的的野马
一直要到跑不动的时候
才会停下来

一匹有才无德的马　饿马
爱跑的马　喜欢懒散而自由地
卧在野地里

看野花的马
累得要死
连草都不想多吃几口的马

你这个人　你老了的时候
成了一匹老马的时候
孤苦伶仃　皮包骨头的马啊

依旧停不下来
依旧是跑啊跑啊
跑个不停

你这匹野马
就是马的命

马的命

The Antique Chinese Zither Made of Aged Wood

She wants to live in an antique Chinese zither.

She does live in an antique Chinese zither.

The zither made of aged wood smells of aged wood scents.

The aged wood's soul thoroughly rid of worms

Is subject to erosions from moon beams and winds alone,

But her solitude and weeping have compensated it.

And if winter comes,

The scents of the aged wood would seep in deep by and by.

An aged zither can readily be coated with dust, and can

Readily pluck clicking sounds of cigarette lighters

And drowsy, monotonous and grotesque melodies.

旧木头做的古琴

她想生活在一架古琴里
她就生活在一架古琴里

旧木头做就的古琴洋溢着旧木头的香味
旧木头的灵魂剔尽了虫子
侵蚀它的只有月光和风
而她的孤独和哭泣却补偿了它

而如果冬天到了
旧木头的香味就会慢慢向深处潜去
一架古琴就喜欢蒙尘　喜欢弹奏出
打火机的嚓嚓声
和令人昏昏欲睡的　干巴而古怪的调子

The Reason I Have an Affection for Glass

I have an affection for glass

For it contains countless acute angles sharper than a knife

Yet not engaged in killing.

I have an affection for shattered glass

For the acute angle each glass fragment represents can not even

Be measured with the aid of planes.

I have an affection for the cracks in the shattered glass

For they are cracks of acute angles beyond measurement,

Are cracks bred with the principle dark clouds spawn lightnings,

Are cracks that only the man who can snatch lightnings

Bare-handed and take it as beauty is able to manipulate

Like manipulating flowers.

我喜欢玻璃的原因

我喜欢玻璃

是其中包含着无数比刀子更尖锐

但却不事杀生的锐角

我喜欢碎玻璃

是每一块碎玻璃所代表的锐角

都无法借助平面去完成丈量

我喜欢碎玻璃上的裂缝

是因为那是无法丈量的锐角的裂缝

是按照乌云酿成闪电的原理而诞生的裂缝

是只有可以徒手搏取闪电并以之为美的人

才能像驾驭花卉一样驾驭的裂缝

North North

My birthplace is in the north. In the north
My fairy cottage is built on the thirsting desert.
Yonder, a flower is so fragile and
Likewise, a lamp is just as fragile.

My birthplace is in the north.
Yonder, my fairy cottage is tender-hearted.
A fragile lamp
And a flower on the verge of extinction
Are two little babies in my fairy cottage.

My fairy cottage is tender-hearted.
It does not loathe the vacant north.
A lamp, a flower at the door,
They are shadows to each other.

My birthplace is in the north
At the knife-tips of the north winds sweeping sand dunes,
At the heart-tips of fairy tales loaded with faint pains.

My birthplace is in the north. I'll tell my fairy tales

Again and again to the north.

I'll let my north gradually grow up in my fairy tales.

北方　北方

我的故乡在北方　北方
我的童话的房屋就建在口渴的沙漠上
那里　一朵花儿有多么懦弱
一盏灯就有多么懦弱

我的故乡在北方
那里，我的童话的房屋是善良的
一盏懦弱的灯
和一朵濒临绝境的花呵
在我的童话的房屋里是两个小宝宝

我的童话的房屋是善良的
它不嫌弃空荡荡的北方
一盏灯　一朵门边的花
它们一个是一个的影子

我的故乡在北方
在北风横扫沙丘的刀尖尖上
在童话的装满隐痛的心尖尖上

我的故乡在北方　我要把我的童话

不断地讲给北方听

我要我的北方在我的童话里慢慢长大

South North

The north in my heart is in fact a kind of water

Squeezed out of stones

Squeezed out of the bodies of men.

I like its unkemptness and

Like it inexplicably

Having itself preserved in the wind.

The south in my heart is also water

And is too much water, too much to handle.

So the water that is somewhat decadent, somewhat muddled is

In places lower than lowlands,

In places where fish can breathe and speak like humans

And can sometimes unknowingly die

With white bellies pointing skyward.

The south   the north

Places I've been to,

One day when I am old, too old to walk,

Eyelids drooping all day,

Are still places I know.

南方　北方

我心中的北方其实是一种水
从石头中挤出来
从男人的身体中挤出来
我喜欢它的不修边幅
喜欢它莫名其妙地
把自己寄存在风中

我心目中的南方也是水
而且是更多的水　多到不可收拾
因而有些颓废也有些迷惘的水
在比低地更低的低处
在鱼可以像人一样呼吸并说话
有时候也肚白朝天
不明真相地死亡的地方

南方　北方
我曾去过的地方
有一天我老了　走不动了
整天耷拉着眼皮
我也知道的地方

The Horse in the Great Wasteland

Standing in the rain

Standing in the great wasteland, the horse

Desolates a whole wild field,

Only the painting of a classic master can be so serene.

The horse stands well aloof from time and the rider,

Well aloof from the muddy grasslands,

Thinking of something.

No one cares a stormy night is on its way,

A night storm more vehement, more overwhelming.

And no one would miss the days when

Father and the horse and irons burning with rage

Jumbled together, flesh and blood.

At rainy moments,

What makes us warm and moist is

The lifetime of the ancient people.

Standing in the rain

Standing in a great wasteland, the horse is

In my vision

Just like awaiting a date in a season of bitter love,

Just like the aristocrat having his home lost,

Just like a kind of beauty beyond imagination.

Just like beyond imagination,

The horse stands on a protruding highland of the cliff

Displaying sunrises and sunsets.

When the sky is teeming with crows

The horse will fall into profound contemplation.

Who is it that

Made the land tattered and displaced?

Who is it that

Compelled us to go farther and farther?

Horses' skeletons attack us from behind in multitudes,

We'll perish into the stones.

马在大荒之中

立于雨中

立于大荒地　马

孤寂了整个一座旷野

只有古典大师的油画才会如此宁静

马是在时间和骑手之外

在泥水的草原之外

构思什么

没有谁关心雨夜将到来

夜雨更猛烈更深沉

也没有谁会怀念

父亲和马和怒火中烧的铁器

血肉相通搅在一起的日子

当雨水的此刻

倍感温暖和湿润的

是古人的一生

立于雨中

立于一片大荒地　马

在我的视野里

如同苦恋季节的一次约会

如同贵族失去了家园
如同想象之外的一种美丽

如同想象之外
马站在崖畔突出的高地上
表现日出日落
等乌鸦注满天空
马便深刻地进入思想

是谁让大地破碎并流离失所
是谁迫使我们走得越来越远
马的骸骨自身后大批袭来
我们将在石头中消失

Imaginary Clock

I imagine myself to be an ancient man
And then I truly become an ancient man
Standing on the threshold.

Some acquaintances and friends
Are deep in the house denying me loudly
And then extolling certain episode in my life.
I hear my aged doddering father
Speaking much of what I want to say,
Then his hoary hairs are on my head. Finally
Dried old hands are reached out one by one from the dusk
To write in Braille about the ancient people's life,
Some doors are being dirtied day by day.

I imagine myself to be an ancient man.
When ceased imagining, buried in the earth,
I am an out-of-date clock.

虚构之钟

我想象自己是古人
就真的成了古人
站在门槛上

一些熟人和朋友
在屋子深处大声否定我
又歌颂我一生中的某个情节
我听到老态龙钟的父亲
说出许多我想说的话
他的白发就上了我的头　最后
苍老之手自黄昏里纷纷伸出
用盲文写着古人的生活
一些门扉被一天天地弄脏

我想象自己是古人
停止想象的时候　埋入土中
我是一口背时的钟

Dense Dark Clouds Hanging Over the Bell Tower[1]

Evening clouds are bending low over the Bell Tower,

Swallows, as if gliding through water playfully in the sky

Trussed up by bandage-like lamp light,

Shuttling up and down like arrows, cruising

As if probing into the khaki-like feline gloomy and lazy twilight

With watery clouds dangling.

Evening clouds bending low, swallows gliding in swarms.

I'm a sleeper, curling up in a feline way on the Bell Tower

On the cement floor behind the marble column,

Encased covertly in a plastic cloth,

A man who dreams of one rain shower

And of attempting to toll the mushroom-like bell

Soaked in the rain.

I also dreamed of a bell ringer with a gray blue glass cat in arms,

Who, after being attacked by clouds and swallows, lingered on,

Pillowing on a huge swath of shards of the gray blue glass cat,

Sleeping in the rainwater throughout the streets,

Dispirited and aggrieved as a discarded object.

钟楼上空乌云密布

晚云在钟楼上空低垂　燕子像戏水一样
在绷带般的灯光所捆绑的天空里
箭一样地上下穿梭　游弋
仿佛是在试探着那灰卡其布似的
猫一样忧郁而慵懒的
垂挂着水淋淋的乌云的夜色

晚云低垂　群燕集翔
我是猫一样蜷缩在钟楼
大理石圆柱背后水泥地上
一个蒙在塑料布里的睡眠者
一个梦见了一场雨
和试图在一口蘑菇一样泡在雨中的钟上
敲出钟声的人

我还梦见了怀抱灰蓝色玻璃猫的敲钟人
被乌云和燕子袭击之后　不忍离去
枕着一大片灰蓝色玻璃猫的碎片
在满大街的雨水中
废弃物般又颓废又委屈地睡眠

The Sound of Bronze

The sound of bronze

Floats far and wide on the rough ground.

My brothers died too many,

Outside of autumn, completing a life of grass,

Outside of a life of grass, still haunting.

My brothers, who is it

That has their faces blown open by the wind

Toward the soul, faces more serene than bronze?

Gone for ever is the earth-shaking snow!

Numerous giant hands reach out of the thick snow,

Painfully striking

The long-silenced world of mortals.

And who is it again in the deep of the sound?

Who is it sitting all the while by the big river

Watching the sun rise and set and the waves

Leap up and then indignantly fall down?

Who is it, in the name of the river bank, that

Makes the soul that cherishes justice and music

Alongside in coexistence with stones when floods arise?

The sound of bronze also comes from the drum.

The second the drum is being stricken,

The two-dimensional soul from

Decayed wood of the ancient times soars up the sky,

Like owls hooting and screeching, like owls

Teeming and shaking the sky, like owls

Standing aloft,

Confined to mountains, enlightened to death.

The sound of bronze, in fact, mostly comes when

A calamity once again demolishes the village.

Initially blooming flowers recede into the dusk,

Initially blooming flowers abruptly languish as passing the dark.

Apart from a modicum of words and belated news,

Mother, son, father, daughter part from each other.

Day and night

A platoon of people get down on the ground painfully crying.

Looking back at the orient,

The sound of bronze is within easy reach.

At the end of the borderland, my brothers

Slowly raise the flags of bronze,

Spread multifarious exclamations in the wind.

Far down deeper than tree roots,

Under the steel and iron piercing the earth,

Stones harder than stones grow higher and higher.

In the wind, my brothers,

Whose sufferings greater than the fish confined in the water,

In an utterly painful mood that water can hardly endure,

Reminisce about the golden soils, brilliant like yellow gold.

青铜之音

青铜之音
在大地和朴素的纵深游曳
我的兄弟死亡太多
在秋天之外完成草的一生
在草的一生之外阴魂不散
我的兄弟，是谁
比青铜更为深沉的面孔迎风吹开
向着心灵，动地的大雪一去不返
众多的巨掌探出大雪之外
疼痛地敲响
久已偃旗息鼓的红尘

是谁又在声音深处
是谁一直坐在大河边上
看日出日落，浪
跳起来又愤怒地落下去
是谁以岸的名义
让热爱正义和音乐的灵魂
大水起时与石头同在

青铜之音还来自鼓

鼓一经敲起来

便有平面的灵魂

自远古的朽木一飞冲天

大枭般啸唱，大枭般

站在高处

不出深山参透而亡

青铜之音其实更多地来自

劫难再一次摧毁村庄

最初开放的花树隐入暮色

最初的花树在越过黑暗时突然凋零

少量的语言与迟到的音讯之外

母子父女相别

朝朝暮暮

一群人伏地痛哭

回首东方

青铜之音近在咫尺

在边土的尽头，我的兄弟

将青铜的旗帜徐徐举起

在大风中传播万端感慨

在比树根更为久远之后

击穿大地的钢铁之下

比石头更为坚硬的石头愈长愈高

在大风中，我的兄弟

苦难胜过伏于水中之鱼

以水难以承受的痛切心境

怀念黄金之土灿若黄金

Notes:

【1】 The Bell Tower（钟楼）: The Bell Tower located in Xi'an（used to be called Chang'an 长安）, the capital of the Shaanxi province in the People's Republic of China, is a stately traditional building that marks the geographical center of the ancient capital. From this important landmark extend East, South, West and North Streets, connecting the tower to the East, South, West and North Gates of the City Wall of the Ming Dynasty（西安明城墙）.

The wooden tower, which is the largest and best-preserved of its kind in China, is 36 meters（118 feet）high. It stands on a square brick base 35.5 meters（116.4 feet）long and 8.6 meters（28.2 feet）high. During the Ming Dynasty, Xi'an was an important military town in Northwest China, a fact that is reflected in the size and historic significance.

The tower was built in 1384 by Emperor Zhu Yuanzhang（朱元璋）as a way to dominate the surrounding countryside and provide early warning of attack by rival rulers.

It has three layers of eaves but only two stories. Inside, a staircase spirals up. The grey bricks of the square base, the dark green glazed tiles on the eaves, gold-plating on the roof and gilded color painting make the tower a colorful and dramatic masterpiece of Ming-style architecture. In addition to enhancing the beauty of the building, the three layers of eaves reduce the impact of rain on the building.

第八辑　海葵花

Part Eight　The Sea Anemone Floweret

The Fish in the South

The fish in the south are streaking in the water.

The fish in the south surfaced glancing at the north.

In a beam of dark blue starlight,

A phantasm-like spider is also streaking,

As if deducing phantasms from phantasms,

As if a dream swiftly replacing

Another dream.

The fish in the south are streaking in the water.

The fish about to spawn cast a glance at the north,

Then the fish tortured by phantasms,

The fish neither howling nor rejoicing,

Begin streaking in the water.

The fish streaking in phantasms,

The fish seeing spiders the minute they glance northward,

Are eagerly seeking the dark shadows which

Need all their scales to be scraped off to pass through.

The fish streaking in the water in the south

Need to rinse out salty flavors lingering in the body.

The inborn beast hide,   the black of spiders,

The black in phantasms

Will by and by turn transparent.

南方的鱼

南方的鱼在水里狂奔

南方的鱼钻出水面望着北方
一束幽蓝的星光下
一只幻影似的蜘蛛也在狂奔
就像幻影在推导幻影
就像一个梦境在迅疾地替代着
另一个梦境

南方的鱼在水里狂奔
将要产卵的鱼　向北一望
就让幻觉折磨的鱼
不嚎叫也不开心的鱼
在水里狂奔

在幻觉中狂奔的鱼
向北一望就看到了蜘蛛的鱼
在水里急切地寻找着
需要刮掉全部鳞片才可穿越的暗影

在南方的水里狂奔的鱼

身体内部尚存的咸味需要洗涤

命中的兽皮　那种蜘蛛的黑

幻觉中的黑

要渐渐变得透明

The Thought of Becoming a Fish

I want to become a fish with personality.

The two legs should become lithe and lissome,
And gradually close up,
And gradually grow into a big tail fin with fishy odors—
I do not refuse the necessary change.

Also necessary are scales from head to toe,
I even deeply adore the attire
Offered by the ocean.

But I'll keep my human eyes.
In the deep ocean, I am a fish,
But I can still use human-like eyes
To eye the ocean, the world of ocean
And the boundless world of fish.

I'll also manage to keep my hands
Even if in the darkness.

Before I desert the coast to be a fish,

I'll use my remaining hands

For the last time to fondle the land I ever resided, the

Land of humans. But in the ocean

I'll use my fish palms

Again and again to stroke

The clouds reflected in the ocean

And the azure blue sky behind the clouds.

I am a fish. I want to say no more.

I no more want to have language.

But I'll use palms to secretly push the waves.

The sound of waves beating against the coasts is

The sound of the ocean,

The sound of the land I resided,

The sound I miss.

I want to become a fish with personality,

A fish maybe seen as a monster in the ocean and in the school

Of fish.

变成一条鱼的构想

我要变成一条有个性的鱼

两腿要变得轻盈
并渐渐合拢
渐渐长成鱼腥味的大大的尾翅——
我不拒绝这起码的变

浑身的鳞甲也不能少
我甚至还深深羡慕着
这大海馈赠的装束

但我要留下我做人的眼睛
在深海里　我是鱼
但我仍然能用人一样的眼睛
打量海　海的世界
和那无边无际的鱼的世界

我还要设法保留我的手
哪怕是在暗处

在我离岸为鱼前

我要用我残存的手

最后一次摸摸我居住过的大地　人

的大地　而在大海里

我要用我鱼的手掌

一遍又一遍地抚摸

映入大海中的云朵

和云朵之后幽蓝的天空

我是鱼　我不想再说什么

不想再有语言

但我要用手掌暗暗地推动波浪

波浪碰击海岸的声音

是大海的声音

是我居住过的大地的声音

我想念的声音

我要变成一条有个性的鱼

一条也许在海里和鱼群里被当作怪物

的鱼

A War Between Humans and Fish

The fish king tells me: In the absence of the moon,

A war will break out between humans and fish.

The fish king

No longer conceals its nationality and identity as a spy.

Its ever-attired scale armors sink buried in the ocean.

It used, in the ocean,

To spit out mouthfuls of salt for water.

The fish king now walks among us

  (*But not in the ocean*)

Looking for water.

Looking for water in lakes

Looking for water in rivers

Looking for water inside the land

Looking for water inside plants and animals.

The fish king walks along with us.

It has mingled among us for ages,

Already conditioned to the smelly odors of the crowds,

Already well acquainted with people's bustling tempo,
Unrefined tastes, insidious acts and idling goodness.

The fish king is just among us.

Beware of this very new-comer, please! The fish king
Asks us for the original ocean, rivers and lakes,
Asks us for the blood inside our bodies,
For the air in the lungs of the shoal,
Including lists of all the deceased from hunger and thirst
On land and throughout dynasties.

The heavy-hearted fish king tells me:
The work does not fare so well. In the absence of the moon,
Between humans and fish
A war may break out.

人鱼之战

鱼王告诉我：月亮不在之时
人和鱼将要爆发战争

鱼王
不再隐瞒国籍和身份的奸细
曾经的鳞甲沉埋大海
曾经在大海中
大口大口地吐盐　求水

鱼王　如今他行走在我们当中
（而不是大海中）
寻找水

寻找湖泊中的水
寻找江河中的水
寻找大地内部的水
寻找植物和动物体内的水

鱼王和我们行走在一起
它打入我们内部　年长日久
已经习惯了人群的腥味

已经太多地掌握了人的忙碌

庸俗、阴险以及无所事事的善良

鱼王就在我们当中

来者不善呵，鱼王

向我们索要曾经的海洋

江河和湖泊　索要我们身体中

的血、鱼群肺部的空气

包括大地上　包括各个朝代

全部饥渴而死的人的名单

忧心忡忡的鱼王告诉我：

工作不太顺利　月亮不在之时

人和鱼

可能要爆发战争

The Seawater on a Sheet of White Paper

The seawater on a sheet of white paper is rioting!

The rioting seawater is the blueness near stars over your head.

Yonder, a white swan's out-of-the-way flight

And its whooping calls are oriented and open as well.

The seawater on a sheet of white paper, the rioting sea,

You should hold it back, should observe the moon's variations,

For it's related to the tides.

White moon   red moon

It's related to the seawater rioting.

The white swan's singing in the azure sky, you patiently wait!

You wait till the singing in the sky comes down!

The singing will again attack the dust and mist repetitively

Ruined by machines and grease stains,

As well as bouts of imperceptible void.

On a sheet of white paper is the rioting seawater,

You should hold it in check.

You should contain that sort of blue that contains pains.

一张白纸上的海水

一张白纸上的海水暴动啦

暴动的海水就是你头顶上方接近星际处的蓝
在那里一只白天鹅偏僻的飞翔
和鸣叫是有方向的　也是开放的

一张白纸上的海水　暴动的海水
你要守住它　要注意观察月亮的变化
因为这与潮汐有关
白月亮　红月亮
这与海水的暴动有关

白天鹅在天空的蓝中的歌唱　你要耐心等待
你要一直等到那天上的歌唱传下来
那歌声将要再次打击
被机器与油污反复毁掉的尘埃迷雾
和　阵阵不易察觉的空虚

一张白纸上　暴动的海水
你要守住
那种内含疼痛的蓝你要守住

Ah! Human-faced Fish

In the pottery jar, there's a pool
Of water streak.
No one can tell clearly
Whether thousands of years' time
Has melted in
Or frozen in it.

On the banks of the ceaseless wailing muddy river,
Mountains were deforming.
In the days under mountains' pressure,
In those shabby cottages and antique caves,
In a place blockaded by spider-webs,
At the bottom of a jar of liquor,
Were the people blurred by years
At mountain ridges and at the ends of the ground.

Deep down inside the last pottery clay
Who was the man in meditation with eyes closed?
Who was the last man crashed into the web?
Who saw the crowd blurred by years
Solitarily walking in dusk,

Rising in the rising blood water,

Approaching stars in the rising flames?

In more profound darkness,

At times, on the hands of wind,

Occasional newspapers reached deep mountains.

On wind hands, the jar without water danced while walking.

In the deeper center of ossification,

After it dropped down,

The overwhelming deluge sounded deeper while sinking.

啊！人面鱼

陶罐里，有一汪

水的线条

谁也说不清

几千年的时光

在其中融化

还是凝固

浑浊号啕不止的大河两岸

大山在变形

大山压着的日子

在那些破茅屋和古窑洞里

在一个被蜘蛛网封锁的地方

在一坛烈酒的底部

是山脊与大地的尽头

那些被日月模糊的人

深入最后的陶土之中

那个闭目沉思的人是谁

最后一个坠毁于网中的人是谁

谁看见被日月模糊的人群

钝钝踽踽的黄昏里

在上升的血水里上升
在上升的火焰里接近星辉

在更深的黑暗中
有时，在风的手掌上
偶尔的报纸抵达大山深处
在风的手掌上无水的陶罐且走且舞
在更深的骨质的中心
在它落下去后，
大水泛滥的声音愈沉愈深

The Sea Anemone Floweret

The water I've never seen, the obscure water,

After the bird and the fox hoaxing each other for a while,

The water no one desires to drink,

At its utmost depths are blooming tiny sea anemone flowerets.

Water (*even obscure water*) in essence is always obscene.

Deeper in water, anemones' round floral plates

Entangled by mucous silk velvet

Are prone to open in the obscurity,

As if the mermaid's one slight absence of sleep

Only glowing a slight gleam.

The water I've never seen, a type of water

I chanced upon on an outing,

Its over-fastidious transparence

Somewhat like the expressions of some deceased soul.

Look down! Look further down!

Beyond mayfly-like messy minute things

Is a tiny anemone floweret.

The water I've never seen is the obscure water.

The flower I can't name seems to be the inflammation infected

By being washed in certain potion in the darkroom,

Emphasizing the gloom in the water by a not very genuine glow.

I call it sea anemone floweret.

海葵花

我从未见过的水　蒙昧之水
鸟和狐狸相互欺骗一番之后
谁也不去喝的水
它的最深处开着小小的海葵花

水（即使是蒙昧之水）的本质总是下流的
在水的更深处　海葵花的圆形花盘
被黏液般的丝绒缠绕着
喜欢在黑暗中张开
仿佛美人鱼一次小小的失眠
只透着一小块的光亮

我从未见过的水　我在一次郊游中
意外地遇到的一种水
它过分讲究的澄澈
那种类似于某种亡魂的神情
往下看　再往下看
越过蜉蝣般纷乱而细小的事物
是一朵小小的海葵花

我从未见到的水是蒙昧之水

我叫不起名字的这种花

仿佛是暗室里某种药水洗出的炎症

它用不太真实的亮丽强调着水中的忧郁

我叫它海葵花

An Encounter with a Mysterious Fish

Water like a bird
Dwells in the stone.
This fish also like a bird
Dwells deep in the stone
Lying in the nest-shaped water.

Right now this fish is nakedly
Scooped out of the stone by me,
Tightly held in the winds and in my hands.

Ah this fish, ferocious-looking like a queer bird
And far too anxiety-provoking!
I don't think I can take it out of the mountains,
Nor do I dare to put it back to the nest-shaped water,
And the mere flash of idea of trying to drop it from high
And sink it down to the unknown abyss
Sets me shedding profuse perspiration.

I remember this fish once surfaced in my dream before
When it was eyeing me with human eyes.
It seemed to have lost its vocal cords,

Its mouth tried to gape but closed, mute as a gargoyle[1].

It reminded me of one night when

A child missing on the way was

Crying almost imperceptibly

In the gloom, indistinctly

Walking all alone.

与一条神奇的鱼相遇

水像鸟一样
居住在石头里
这条鱼也像鸟一样
居住在石头深处
那卧作鸟巢状的水里

此时这条鱼赤条条地
被我从石头里掏出来
拈在风里和手里

这有着怪鸟一样凶险的长相
而又令人思虑重重的鱼呵
我想我不能把它带出山中
也不敢让它再回到鸟巢状的水里
而试图将它扔下高处
沉入未知深渊的想法
刚一闪念就让我禁不住虚汗大发

我记得这条鱼早先曾在梦中出现
当时它用人一样的目光看着我
它像丧失了声带一样

嘴巴欲张又拢　一声不吭
让我想起一天夜里
一个失踪在路上的孩子
不易察觉地哭泣着
在黑暗中　若隐若现
一个人独自行走

The Birth of Water

In the boundless sea,

Not a single drop of water is to be found.

Oh! My last one child!

Today, I make my first hand sign,

Beckoning you, in the billowing waves,

To come with the water,

Toward the seashore where I stand.

In those years, child!

I all the time sailed far out to sea

In the winds and tempests,

At the meeting point of the sky and the water,

Experiencing ups and downs, carrying me along, seeking me.

In those years, child!

It was a woman telling me while crying.

She heard the door-knocking in my body,

Forced me to brutally smash her door,

Letting out a long-lost growl of beast.

Then, I finally found myself,

It was you crying deep in the sea.

Oh! My last child! Today

The sea is on the brink of dyke breaching,

Crimson red blood is flooding without a stop,

You're rising and falling with the waves,

That woman and I

Can't refrain from wailing bitterly.

Child! The tempest will die off soon.

My ship is already stranded

On the shore where we can't go on sailing.

I face the sea making hand signs,

Bellowing loud at you to lap and slap waves.

Listen! Child!

Come along with the water!

Come to my side!

Stay by my side!

Light a bonfire!

Let me ooze warmly out from depths

Like smoke rising over the back of fire.

Let me from a very very high place

Shine upon you along with the water, overflowing the land.

Listen! My last child!

I loudly shout to you,

Shout you to come along with the water,

To go along with the water,

And on the global surface burned by the ancestors

Rebuild a tide-like gracefully-rhythmed homestead.

水的诞辰

茫茫大海
寻找不到一滴水
我的最后一个孩子啊
今天，我做出第一个手势
示意你在波涛汹涌中
朝着我站立的海岸
随水而来

那些年月，孩子
我一直出海远航
在大风和暴雨中
在水天掺合处
历尽坎坷带着我寻找我

那些年月，孩子
是一个女人哭着告诉我
她听到我身体里响着敲门声
迫使我残酷地打碎她的门
发出一种业已消失的兽鸣
于是，我终于找到了自己
是你在大海深处哭喊

我的最后一个孩子啊，今天
大海濒临破碎决堤
殷红的血泊泛滥不已
你随波逐流
我和那个女人
禁不住痛哭失声

孩子，风暴不久将过去
我的船也已搁浅
在不能继续前行的岸上
我面向大海做着手势
纵声呼喊你拍击波涛

听着！孩子
随水而来
来到我身旁
守在我身旁
打起篝火
让我从深处温热地流出
像烟雾从火脊上腾起
让我在很高很高的地方
照着你随水漫过大地

听着！我的最后一个孩子
我大声呼喊你
呼喊你随水而来

随水而去
在祖宗焚化的球面上
重建潮水般韵律优美的家园

Oh! Water

My river is ageing,

Fatigued and outraged,

Flowing through the deep canyon.

Oh! The fatigued and outraged water

Flows roaring for thousands upon thousands of miles.

Flies, one after another,

Transform into fish one after another

Sucking the rushing torrents.

Oh! The fatigued and outraged water!

Many ships are setting out,

Cutting through waves.

Many ships are sailing off the village,

Miserable for seeking nets.

Oh water, from the boundless billowy mountains!

Oh waves, like chains of mountains never transparent!

Many nameless skeletons pile up on river beds,

Deep-set eye sockets, mossy and glossy,

Pierce through the turbidity month after month, year after year.

Oh water! Centuries have elapsed,

Another few centuries have elapsed.

My river is ageing,

Mountains, rivers, and the land are starkly impoverished.

Today, every patch with grass grown on is

The auspicious skin of the earth.

水啊

我的河流在老化
它疲倦而愤怒地
从大峡谷深处流过

疲倦而愤怒之水啊
一泻千里的喧啸
一只只苍蝇
变成一条条大鱼
啜饮激流

疲倦而愤怒之水啊
许多船出发了
割着波涛
许多船驶离村庄
为寻找网而凄苦

水啊！来自波涛似无边际的群山
波涛啊！群山一样永不澄清
许多无名骷髅累积河底
深邃的眼眶苔藓依依
年年月月洞穿浑浊

水啊！几个世纪过去了

又几个世纪过去了

我的河流在老化

山河大地一贫如洗

今天，长出草丛的

每一块都是土地般吉祥的皮肤

Lighthouse

Like a young mother's prematurely wrinkled face, lighthouse
Red, tender and plain
No more twinkles over the sea of the olden times.

Starting from the internal plot of life,
Starting from certain everlasting darkness,
Having brilliancy of the thing itself
And affection aloft, in a prominent position
At the sea in extreme starvation and thirst you pass by at times,
Oh! Lighthouse! You no longer shine
Into the ominous and hollow blue
In the distance of sea.

Perhaps I am merely an onlooker.
Perhaps the lighthouse is changing directions—

Oh! Lighthouse! Shine in the heart of stones
Like a spider secluded deep down the burrows!
Shine in the lung of the ground!
Shine behind one star that extinguished
Just now!

灯塔

像年轻母亲早逝的祥容　灯塔
红嫩而简朴的灯塔
已不在昔日的海上闪烁

从生命的内部情节开始
从某种持续的黑暗开始
带着事物本身的光芒
和高高在上的爱意
在你偶尔路过而饥渴难耐的海上
灯塔呵，已不再照耀
大海远方
凶险而空洞的蓝

也许我仅仅是个观望者
也许灯塔正在转移方向——

灯塔呵，在石头的内心点亮
像地穴中深居简出的蜘蛛
在大地的肺部点亮
在天空中一颗刚才熄灭的星星背后
点亮

Notes:

【1】Gargoyle（怪兽状滴水嘴）： The word gargoyle is derived from an old French word gargouille（音译："嘎咕鬼"，意为"喉咙"或"食道"）meaning throat. The English word gargle is derived from the same word. Originally a gargoyle was considered a waterspout, directing water away from a building. Technically an architect calls a waterspout（喷水口）on a building a gargoyle. If a stone carving does not carry water and has a face that resembles a creature, it is technically called a grotesque. A strange beast which combines several different animals is called a chimera.

Many people believe that gargoyles were developed by medieval architects and stone carvers to ward off evil in an imperfect world. Whatever their purpose, they adorn countless cathedrals in the world. They've inspired curiosity, awe, laughter, and occasionally fear. Some say the first known reference dates back to 600 A.D.

France has over 100 cathedrals, most built in the middle ages, with Notre Dame （巴黎圣母院）being the most famous. It's true that in the Middle ages, the populace, for the most part, couldn't read and write. Churches used awesome visual images to spread the scriptures, such as gargoyles, stained glass, and sculpture. Some believe that gargoyles were inspired directly via a passage in the bible. Others believe that gargoyles and grotesques do not come from the bible, but are inspired by the skeletal remains of prehistoric beasts such as dinosaurs and giant reptiles. Others will argue that they are the expression of man's subconscious fears or, that they may be vestiges of paganism from an age when god would be heard in trees and river plains. Know, also, that the churches of Europe carried them further into time; maybe to remind the masses that "even if god is at hand, evil is never far away..." or "possibly to act as guardians of their church to keep the terrible spirits of evil away."

第九辑　雕像与城

Part Nine　The Statue and the City

Heterogeneity

A crow and a fox,

One is on the bough,

The other is below the tree.

The crow likes practicing bel canto[1]singing at the sight of the fox;

The fox just wants to exhibit oral stunts at the sight of the crow.

A crow and a fox

Are heterogeneous yet clear about each other's hidden-secrets;

After vying for cleverness at singing and slick-talking,

Henceforth, they live far apart.

异类

一只乌鸦　和一只狐狸
一个在树枝上
一个在树底下

乌鸦见了狐狸喜欢练练美声
狐狸瞅见乌鸦就想演演口技

一只乌鸦和一只狐狸
两个互知隐情的异类
用歌唱和花言巧语比赛一番聪明之后
从此天各一方

The Silent Man

The silent man
Himself carelessly planted the supreme part of his vocal cord
In the field.

The silent man
Stays perceptive that restraint on speech brings good luck,
Stays perceptive how much a tree growing increasingly taller
Favors rainwater.

The silent man
Stays perceptive that those flamboyant voices are made of paper,
They are derived from the savage tree-felling,
Thus dreading rainwater.

The silent man
Retires at home way prior to the due time
Trimming and watering flowers in the orchard,
Roaming in the groves on hillocks,
Seeming like a gardener lost in the dream.

沉默的人

沉默的人
他把自己声带上最好的一个部位
不慎种进了地里

沉默的人
知道克制语言会使人幸运
知道一棵越长越高的树
多么喜欢雨水

沉默的人
知道那些华丽的声音是纸做的
它们来自暴行般的砍伐
因而害怕雨水

沉默的人
不到时候就早早退休回家
在化园里剪枝　　浇花
在有树林子的山上转悠
像一个遗失在梦里的园丁

The Symbolist's Summer

The man clad in pitch-black shiny fish scales,

The man head-dressed in an ox's horn,

The man whose loin wrapped with a spotted boa constrictor

The man claiming for toxicants from the moon,

The man having deposited the whole nightmare processing mill

On the comet,

The man having brought incantations by reticent solo walking

All are the men I've never before seen

With eerie expressions.

象征主义者的夏天

身披黑亮鱼鳞的人
头饰牛角的人
腰缠花斑蟒蛇的人

向月亮索取毒药的人
在彗星上寄存了整座噩梦加工厂的人
用沉默的独行带来符咒的人

都是我从未见过的
表情怪异的人

Upward and Downward

A mountain is upward

   (*This is the reason I don't give it up*) .

A forest is upward

   (*This is the reason the land doesn't give it up*) .

A piebald hunting leopard, like lightning,

Shuttles to and fro in the dim forest. This unerringly apt hostility

Also is upward.

It makes some timid and tiny things

Have to hide deeper or escape to somewhere higher.

In lightnings or in icy snows, it tempers

The laws of survival and the skills of running under the sun.

In the howls of wolves and roars of tigers,

Even death is upward.

Everything buried underground is

Interlinked to root systems. Down there

Death recklessly joins into other lives, and then

With only white bones left, like souls refreshed in places deeper,

Re-emerges fresh, beautiful and spirited.

The land is upward, the forest is upward, the dust is upward.

Animals and nutrients in the forest,

In the form of death and mutual annihilation, are upward.

The sun seems to be downward.   The moon,

Imitator's paragon, is also downward.

But the expansive dust in the light beam,

Its silence and stillness by virtue of being too light,

By virtue of being closer to the essence,

Carrying along the core of light inside the light,

Is absolutely upward.

向上的和向下的

山是向上的

（这是我不放弃它的理由）

森林是向上的

（这是大地不放弃它的理由）

一只花斑猎豹像闪电一样

穿梭着森林的幽暗，这恰如其分的敌意

也是向上的

它使一些胆怯和渺小的事物

必须藏得更深或者逃向更高处

在闪电或冰雪中　锤炼

生存下去的法则　和在太阳底下奔跑的本领

在狼嚎虎啸之中

甚至连死也是向上的

一切埋在地底的东西

都和根系连在一起　那里

死亡大手大脚地　加入另外的生命

然后只剩下白骨　像灵魂在更深处完成了脱胎换骨

出落得干净　美丽　神采奕奕

大地向上　森林向上　尘埃向上
森林中的动物和养料
以死和相互湮灭的形式　向上

太阳仿佛是向下的　　月亮
模仿者的楷模也是向下的
但那光束中广阔的尘埃
它的沉默和寂静　由于太轻
由于更接近本质
它在光中携带着光的中心
是绝对向上的

Three Maxims

The violence clothed in brightly-colored clothes
Breaks the single one mirror
Just before leaving the house.

The pane bound in handcuffs,
When passing by a window smelling of decay,
Practices ogling.

In the wake of dissection of a corpse with a psychosis history,
There's found a large mass of ash of bleaching powder unabsorbed
And a large mass of penicillin crystals un-dissolved.

三句箴言

穿着花衣服的暴力
临出门前
打碎唯一一面镜子

戴手铐的玻璃
经过一扇发出腐败味道的窗户时
练习抛媚眼

具有精神病史的尸体被解剖后
发现了大量未吸收的漂白粉般的灰烬
和大量未溶解的青霉素结晶体

Anonymous Letter of Authorization

Return the sky to eagles

And golden-rumped swallows.

Return the pine-wood to south winds and north winds.

Return the golden coastlines to the seas.

Return the blind man's harp twangs to the skeletons and dynasties

Buried undersea, and to Homer[2],

The man drowned by the forlorn sea.

Return my body to the god of war and the god of wit

In cartoon fiction films.

Return languages to the man who kissed the demise

As if kissing an infant.

Return the mirror carelessly broken last year to a freeze factory.

Return the moon to water-wells.

无名氏授权书

把天空还给鹰

和胡燕

把松木还给南风和北风

把黄金的海岸线还给海水

把盲人的琴声还给葬身海底的骸骨和朝代

还给荷马

这被孤苦伶仃的海水淹死的人

把我的身体还给卡通故事片中

的战神和智慧之神

把语言还给那个亲吻死亡

如同亲吻婴孩的人

把去年不慎打碎的一面镜子还给冷冻加工厂

把月亮还给水井

The Castle on the Border

Send the Czar[3] in the dream into exile here

A place where forefathers flogging galloping horses by
Scattered the bleached bones of their foes and of their own.
Send deserts, prairies and damaged pails into exile here.

It's a place teeming with jade-like bleak starlight,
With cries of she-wolf Joanna [4] and epidemic diseases.
Send snowstorms of languages into exile here.

Send moralists, preachers
And their gunpowder mills into exile here.

边境上的城堡

把梦中的沙皇流放在这里

打马狂奔的先人　散尽仇人
和自己白骨的地方
把沙漠、草原和毁坏的水桶流放在这里

充满了凄厉如玉的星光
和母狼胡安娜带来号哭与传染病的地方
把语言的暴风雪流放在这里

把道德家　说教者
和他们的火药工厂流放在这里

Two Still Things

A pair of scissors and a mirror

Are held in the same man's hands at the same time,

His (*a man's*) livid countenance

Contains intense eyes some animal can have.

A pair of scissors and a mirror,

One on the left, one on the right.

The faces they like to reveal in the firelight and sunlight,

Are two sharply discrepant faces.

A pair of scissors and a mirror

Are cool and calm in the hands of a man,

Are moist and lukewarm in the hands of a woman,

Are prone to rust and fester in dusty winds.

But in my hands, a pair of scissors and a mirror,

They are similar to two props with hesitating temperaments,

With genders faintly looming, with vivid colors drooping,

As though hard to assuredly find the direction of might.

两个静物

一把剪子和一面镜子
被同一个男人同时拿在手里
他（一个男人）的铁青的面容
暗合着某类动物才有的深邃目光

一把剪子和一面镜子
一个在左边　　一个在右边
它们喜欢在火光和日光里显现的面孔
是两种截然不同的面孔

一把剪子和一面镜子
在一个男人手里是冷静的
在一个女人手里是潮热的
在夹杂着尘埃的风里是可以生锈或溃烂的

但在我的手里　　一把剪子和一面镜子
它们类似于性格犹疑的两个道具
拥有时隐时现的性别　　热烈的颜色奄拉着
仿佛难以确定发现力量的方向

Naturalist

If to write of a steelbar piercing a construction worker's chest,
I'd refer to magma and its secret pores in deep internal flames.

If to write of monster-like thriving cities and building clusters,
I'd refer to nameless mountain and the celestial dog swallowing
the moon[5] as if eating a pancake above it.

If to write of the car exhaust fume and smog,
I'd refer to cows shitting in villages for overeating poppy in the
old society.

If to write of a dump piled with shattered glass, worn-out leather
and waste plastic,
I'd refer to the man who ate arsenic trioxide and a scale weight
Lying like a crow dead in a sprawl in the wildness.

自然主义者

如果我要写钢筋穿透了建筑工人的胸腔
我就写岩浆和它内部火焰深处的秘密气孔

如果我要写怪物般生长的城市和楼群
我就写无名的山脉和它上面吃煎饼一样吞月的天狗

如果我要写汽车尾气和雾霾
我就写旧社会吃多了罂粟的牛在村庄里拉屎

如果我要写堆积着碎玻璃、旧皮革和废塑料的垃圾场
我就写吃了砒霜和秤砣的人
像乌鸦一样四脚朝天死在旷野上

The Statue and the City

The city can't read the statue

Standing in its square

As if the human heart is so crowded

Yet can find nowhere to stand,

As if in the winds and in the rains,

In the smoke and in the fog,

The statue stands speechless.

O the statue! A hero through slayings on ancient pathways.

He banished war horses and swords to a foreign land of time.

People banished him into the center of stone

In the grand square of the city. O the statue!

Nostalgic beyond desires as far as the cosmic horizon,

Tears blown dry by winds.

The city is doomed to be a logic,

Too many people,

Too many mouths,

Needless to narrate.

Upon my looking afar to the other bank of the huge river,

Those friends are still expecting the tidings.

I am, in a place with none around, yelling again and again

 "Stay where you are!"

雕像与城

城市读不懂雕像
在自己的广场

犹如人心拥挤
却找不到驻足的地方
犹如风里雨里
烟里雾里
雕像无语

雕像呵，这古道上杀出的英雄
他把战马和宝剑流放时间的异乡
众人把他流放在石头的中央
在城市巨大的广场上，雕像呵
高于欲望的怀想远及天际
大风把泪水吹干

城市注定是一种逻辑
人太多
嘴太多
无须记叙

遥望大河彼岸

那些朋友还在等候消息

我在没人的地方一次次大喊

先别来

Notes:

[1] Bel canto（美声）：Bel canto (Italian, "beautiful singing" or "beautiful song"), is an Italian musical term relating to Italian singing. It refers to the art and science of vocal technique which originated in Italy during the late 16th century and reached its pinnacle in the early part of the 19th century during the bel canto opera era. Bel canto singing characteristically focuses on perfect evenness throughout the voice, skillful legato, a light upper register, tremendous agility and flexibility, and a certain lyric, "sweet" timbre.

The words (bel canto) were not associated with a "school" of singing until the middle of the 19th century, when writers in the early 1860s used it nostalgically to describe a manner of singing that had begun to wane around 1830. Nonetheless, "neither musical nor general dictionaries saw fit to attempt a definition of bel canto until after 1900". The term remains vague and ambiguous in the 21st century and is often used to evoke a lost singing tradition.

[2] Homer（荷马）：Homer is Homeros in Greek for hostage. He was a legendary early Greek poet traditionally credited with writing the major Greek epics *The Iliad* and *The Odyssey*（《伊利亚特》和《奥德赛》）.

Tradition depicts Homer as a blind minstrel wandering from place to place reciting poems that had come down to him from a very old oral tradition. Many scholars believe that the books as they exist today were not written by a single person and were not put in writing until centuries after they took their present form.

It is probable that much of the epic tradition of the two books was formed in the 200 or 300 years before an alphabet reached Greece in the 9th or 8th century B.C. If so, it is possible that Homer used earlier writings to help him, or he could have dictated his poems to someone else because of his blindness or because he was illiterate.

[3] Czar（沙皇）: The term czar is a Russian equivalent of the Roman title Caesar（恺撒）. Before the 1917 revolution in Russia, the emperor or ruler was called the czar. The last czar was czar Nicholas II（沙皇尼古拉二世）, who abdicated for himself and his son in 1917. He and his family were killed by the Bolsheviks（布尔什维克）afterwards. Vladimir Illich Ulyanov（弗拉基米尔·伊利奇·乌里扬诺夫）, later known as Lenin（列宁）took control as a Bolshevik leader.

[4] She-wolf Joanna（母狼胡安娜）: She-wolf Joanna might be a term coined by the poet Yan An, which evokes us recollections of two most tragic women in the history:

Joanna of Castile 胡安娜（卡斯蒂利亚）（1479—1555）, known as Joanna the Mad（Spanish: Juana la Loca/ 疯女胡安娜）, was queen of Castile from 1504 and of Aragon from 1516.

Isabella of France 伊莎贝拉（法兰西）（1295—1358）, as a princess of France used to be named Isabella the Fair（法兰西第一美人）because of her beauty. She was one of the most powerful, reviled and tragic women in European history. For her audacity, her wit, and her cunning, she came to be maligned for centuries as she-wolf of France（法兰西母狼）.

Thomas Gray 托马斯·格雷（1716—1771）, English poet whose *An Elegy Written in a Country Church Yard*（《乡村墓园挽歌》或《墓畔哀歌》）is one of the best known of English lyric poems also depicted she-wolf of France in his poem The Bard -Pindaric Ode（游吟诗人 - 品达罗斯颂歌）: "she-wolf of France, with unrelenting fangs, That tear'st the bowels of thy mangled mate."

[5] The celestial dog swallowing the moon（天狗吞月）: The story of the celestial dog swallowing the moon or Tian Gou Tun Yue is a well- known mythology to all Chinese. The mythology is delivering this as a celestial demon, which has a huge mouth and a voracious appetite that would swallow everything, including the moon and the sun. This phenomenon is what we know today in astronomy as the eclipse.

第十辑　对峙之美

Part Ten　Beauty of Confrontation

White Snow Descending, Red Plums Blooming

The lonely snow is flying over the lonely dark clouds,

Flying in the north, flying above dark clouds in the north,

En route to the sea,

All the way to south without obstruction, flying in the south.

Dark clouds are flying, white snow descending in profusion,

Descending in the south and in the north,

Descending in the whole world.

The white of one boundless expanse of white snow,

I know the Pacific Ocean needs it, you need it,

An eagle and eagle-like steel aircraft also need it.

A kind of emphatically descending temperature calculator,

A kind of white concerning bared lips and cold teeth,

The white of white snow descending in profusion,

Dark clouds need it,

The world and its fleecy messy white need it,

The red concerning red lips and white teeth needs it.

White snow descending, red plums blooming.

I know in places without snow

The blooming red plum trees are in silence,

Likewise, the blooming white plum trees are in silence.

Dark clouds are flying, white snow descending,

Descending above the sea, descending

At the ends of the world, at the depths of the sleeping world.

White snow descending, red plums blooming

White plum flowers fluffy like white snow

Are also blooming.

白雪向下　红梅怒放

孤独的雪在孤独的乌云上飞奔

在北方飞奔　在北方的乌云上飞奔

去大海的路上

一路南下毫无遮拦　在南方飞奔

乌云飞奔，白雪纷纷下落

在南方和北方下落

在全世界下落

一场漫无边际的白雪的白

我知道太平洋需要　你需要

一只鹰和类似于鹰的钢铁的飞行器也需要

一种强调性下行的温度计算器

一种事关唇亡齿寒的白

白雪纷纷下落的白

乌云需要

世界和它毛茸茸的散乱的白需要

唇红齿白的红需要

白雪向下　红梅怒放

我知道没有雪的地方

怒放的红梅树是沉默的

同样怒放的白梅树也是沉默的

乌云飞奔　白雪下落

在大海上下落

在世界尽头睡眠的世界深处下落

白雪向下　红梅怒放

白雪一样蓬松的白色的梅花

也怒放

The Blue Lakes in the North

Through boundless yellow sands and countless mountains,
The blue lakes are then in sight;
That is a place where stars shine like lamplight
Every day waiting for the fall of night.

The stones solely in northern existence and in our ignorance
Are dotting the lakesides like star signs, as if stars' remains
Were waiting for the stars in the lakes to shine, and
Then they'd, like seeing long lost kins, gaze in consternation,
Secretly sobbing without any explanation.

I believe the lakes are also waiting for my appearance,
Waiting for my coming not on aircraft but on foot alone,
Coming not in the prime of life but on foot all my life,
Coming wobbling along not until almost too senile to stride.

How lonely the lights in northern blue lakes brightened by stars!
How lonely the huge stones like star signs beside lakes are!
They're waiting for my coming, for me to enter twilight of life,
Unable to be anywhere except to let lights by the lakesides and
The stars in long deep sleep on the hearts of huge stones

Together brighten.

北方那些蓝色的湖泊

越过黄沙万里　山岭万重
就能见到那些蓝色的湖泊
那是星星点灯的地方
每天都在等待夜幕降临

那些只有北方才有的不知来历的石头
在湖边像星座一样分布　仿佛星星的遗骸
等着湖泊里的星星点灯之后
他们将像见了失散多年的亲人一样面面相觑
不由分说偷偷哭泣一番

我相信那些湖泊同样也在等待我的到来
等待我不是乘着飞行器　而是一个人徒步而来
不是青年时代就来　而是走了一辈子路
在老得快要走不动的时候才蹒跚而来

北方蓝色湖泊里那些星星点亮的灯多么寂寞
湖边那些星座一样的巨石多么寂寞
它们一直等待我的到来　等待我进入垂暮晚境
哪儿也去不了　只好把岸边的灯
和那些在巨石心脏上沉睡已久的星星

一同点亮

The Birds of the Whole World Are Flying into Dusk

The cities of the whole world are expanding to the suburb,

The birds of the whole world are flying into dusk in the suburb.

Lucky is yon peach plum pond enclosed by a bamboo grove,

Lucky is yon waste land shrouded by a more lush tree grove,

It's a place where the birds of the whole world prefer in dusk

To meet with their blood kins and kinfolks

Where the verdant tree grove and bamboo grove

Occupy swathes of cropland and deserted lands of villages,

A place having expelled swarms of population and inhabitants,

A barren region half hidden and half adorned by groves.

Countless shadow-like birds, like countless dark shreds,

Fly out of the dusk blotting out the sky and the land

In the peculiar gloom of the suburb and groves,

As if staging an uprising, seething with excitements.

The birds of the whole world are flying into the dusk.

The suburb deeply occupied by tree grove and bamboo grove

Has no spires to entangle with,

Has no moon to intertwine with.

A huge swarm of birds seems freshly awakened,

Seems to try to awaken the whole suburb, the whole groves

And its whole waste land and

The desolation in the dark

And take them elsewhere.

全世界的鸟都飞向黄昏

全世界的城市都向郊区扩张

全世界的鸟都飞向郊区的黄昏

那里有幸被竹林子包围着的桃花潭

有幸被更茂盛的树林子笼罩的旷野

是全世界的鸟选择黄昏

去会见亲人和亲戚的地方

青翠的树林子和竹林子

占据了大片的庄稼地和村庄的撂荒地

一个赶走了大批人口和住户的地方

一个用树林子半是掩盖半是装饰的荒凉地带

无数阴影般的鸟　像无数个黑暗的碎片

它们铺天盖地从黄昏中飞来

在郊区和树林子特有的幽暗中

像要发动一场起义似的沸腾着

全世界的鸟都飞向黄昏

被树林子和竹林子深深占领的郊区

没有塔尖可以缠绕

也没有月亮可以缠绵的郊区

巨大的鸟群仿佛刚刚醒来一样

仿佛要把整个郊区、整个树林子

和它的全部旷野

在黑暗中的荒凉全部叫醒

带向另外的地方

In MuUs[1], Meeting a Shepherd Aged into Unconsciousness

A desert paler than a dead fish's belly,
A desert paler than saline-alkali
Now is living in his ears,
Living in his eyes,
Living in his sweat pores,
Living in his throat.

The sun-dried old flesh of his body is
Too dry to squeeze out a single droplet of oil.
Like a clothes-hanger, his old bones
Can not yet stately hold up
The flesh hanging down like a heap of rags.
Before he could tell me anything, he commenced to cough
Yet the voice delved into his tiniest shriveled lung and
Could not be scooped out even by a knife.

The old man that stood facing the wind later only coughed
Just enough to produce a tiny tear,
A tear that could not even moisten secretions in the eyes.
And then in a wave of trance, my tears
Like well-water welled up inside my body.

毛乌素，偶遇老得失去知觉的牧者

比死鱼肚子还苍白的沙漠
比盐碱还苍白的沙漠
如今住在他的耳朵里
住在他的眼睛里
住在他的汗毛孔里
住在他的喉咙里

被太阳榨干的一身老肉皮
再也榨不出一滴油水
一副衣架似的老骨头
已无法堂皇地撑起
那一堆破布片般向下披挂的皮囊
他还没有告诉我什么，就开始出声咳嗽
但那声音钻入已经萎缩到最小的肺里
用刀子掏也掏不出来了

迎风而立的老人　后来只咳出一滴细微的泪水
一滴让眼角屎都无法湿润的泪水
还有一阵恍惚之中　我的
像井水一样在身体内部弥漫的泪水

The Apron Blue of Celestial Hue

The woman scythed grass and scythed the sun

on hills all her life,

The woman scythed grass to breed livestock,

and scythed the sun to feed us,

The woman dyed cloth with the sap of grass and trees

and sewed clothing for us,

The woman cleansed the decayed wood

and sludge by the Yellow River[2],

The woman delivered water in a pottery jar to father

and to the blazing sun atop of hills,

The woman dyed white cloth into black, blue, red, green cloth

and heavily dressed up the desolate years,

The woman in a place where the sky is bluer than

the apron blue of celestial hue,

All her life murmured sons' and daughters' infant names,

yet forgetting to chant ballads herself,

The woman atop of hills watched bird flocks and the setting sun

fade into boundless mountains,

Last year I returned to my birthplace and

planted grasses for her grave mound,

This year I returned to my birthplace and

planted trees for her grave mound,

Next year I'll return to my birthplace and give the sky and her

apron blue of celestial hue a cautious dyeing

One more time in her invented way of dyeing white cloth.

Mother, the paradise too remote, the world even more remote,

But our tears, skeletons and ashes

Will be scattered or gathered like dusty winds by strange lands.

Some day, your apron blue of celestial hue

Will also be covered with dust and dead twigs.

The enclosures and the sky you left behind no longer

Have anyone to give a dyeing to, and will by and by turn white,

As white as empty,

As empty as white.

天空色的围裙蓝

那个在山上终生割草割太阳的女人

那个割草喂牲口　割太阳喂我们的女人

那个用草木的汁液染布给我们缝衣服的女人

那个在黄河边上洗涤朽木和污泥的女人

那个用陶罐给山顶上的父亲和烈日送水的女人

那个把白布染成黑布、蓝布、红布、绿布

重重地装饰荒凉年代的女人

那个在天空比天空色的围裙蓝还蓝的地方

终生念叨儿女的乳名却忘记了唱歌的女人

那个在山顶上看着鸟群和夕阳沉入苍茫群山的女人

去年我回到故乡　给她的墓地种了草

今年我回到故乡　给她的墓地种了树

明年我还将回到故乡

把天空和她的天空色的围裙蓝

用她生前发明的洗染白布的方法

小心翼翼地再染一遍

母亲　天堂太远　尘世更远

而我们的眼泪　尸骨和灰烬

将被异乡像风尘一样散落或者收敛

有朝一日　你的天空色的围裙蓝

也将落满风尘和枯枝

你留下的围墙和天空

再也无人染色　将渐渐发白

白得一无所有

空空如也

The Mediterranean[3]

Today I'll write about the Mediterranean,
The Mediterranean some more refugee ships capsized in,
The Mediterranean plenty more women, kids and sad-eyed men
Were dumped in like rotten fish and shrimps to feed the fish.

Of the seas in the world, the most famed is the Mediterranean.
It's the Mediterranean, booming ceaselessly, holding up the
Blind poet Homer's seven-stringed lyre and the secrets of the Sea
god Poseidon's[4] single-handed battle with seas over waves.
The seas of the world all contain deaths, abysses and
Ecstasy soups that make dead souls struck with disorientation.
The Mediterranean initiated with gods chasing one another,
Bronze and rocks together slash and polish the ancient coasts.
The people scorched by fires and soaked by floods in homeland,
Ships and people sailing away from homeland like defectors,
Today once more sink onto the seabed in heaps of dead bones;
Warships, planes see none of their vulnerability and desperation.

Today I'll write about the Mediterranean,
Which is a tomb in time,
Is Europe's blood, is one basin of cold blood
With Homer's and gods' incisors knocked out
And with the time's incisors knocked out.

地中海

今天我要写到地中海
又有几艘难民船倾覆其中的地中海
又有很多妇女　儿童和眼神忧郁的男人
像烂鱼虾一样倒入海中喂鱼的地中海

全世界的大海　鼎鼎有名的要数地中海
把盲诗人荷马的七弦琴
和海神波塞冬与大海单打独斗的秘籍
举在波浪上轰鸣不止的大海是地中海
全世界的大海都包含着死亡　深渊
和令亡魂们丧失方向的迷魂汤
地中海　从诸神相互追逐开始
青铜和岩石一起打磨着古老的海岸
那些在祖国被火灾烤过被水灾泡过的人
那些像叛逃一样驶离祖国的轮船和人
今天又一次尸骨累累沉积海底
军舰和飞机再也看不到他们的小和绝望了

今天我要写到的地中海
是一个时间中的坟墓
是欧洲的血　是磕掉了荷马和诸神门牙
也磕掉了时间门牙的一盆子冷血

Confucius[5] Must Have Seen the Sea

Confucius must have seen the sea,

No wonder he was keen on riding horses and donkeys.

All his life walking along the edges of rivers,

Without ever asking fish or asking dragons,

He is already aware of the secret why every river flows

Desperately toward the sea as if toward death.

Confucius must have seen the sea,

No wonder he was keen on climbing Mount Tai[6],

Keen on, at the peak of Mount Tai, the eastern sacred mountain,

Having a bird's-eye view of floating clouds of all ages and

Embracing mountains and rivers looming below clouds,

Like silk, like clay balls, like rain drops, like dew.

Confucius must have seen the sea,

No wonder he could see flying birds, could see floating clouds,

Could also see, behind cloud-like flying birds and

Bird-like floating clouds,

The cloud-like grounds and all the cloud-like hazy things

Like floating clouds, vaguely flickering and looming.

Hey! The man named Confucius,

Whose hair on bald head blown frantically by gales all along

Would soon collapse like blighted seaweeds,

I guess he must have seen the sea.

孔子一定见过大海

孔子一定见过大海

所以他才喜欢乘马骑驴

终生沿着大河的边际行走

没有问过鱼　也没有问过龙

就通晓了为什么每一条河流

赴死般不顾一切奔赴大海的秘密

孔子一定见过大海

所以他喜欢登临泰山

喜欢在东岳泰山的绝顶上

俯瞰　将万世浮云尽收眼底

将浮云之下　丝绸泥丸般若有若无的山河

像雨滴露水一样收入胸中

孔子一定见过大海

因此他看得见飞鸟　看得见浮云

也看得见在浮云似的飞鸟

和飞鸟似的浮云之后

那像浮云般若隐若现和若有若无的

云层般的大地以及云层般渺茫的万物

嗨！这个名叫孔子的人
他秃顶上的毛发被劲风一直狂吹着
像快要枯死的海藻一样一蹶不振
我猜想他一定见过大海

Floating Clouds Chart

Look up! The traces dropped by floating clouds

Frightened away a flying bird's one-day flight

And an ant's one lifetime beyond man's sight.

At the crags attainable only by flight

Are cypresses, pines and nameless vines

That can grow without earth,

Only winds know their dew condensed in the fogs,

And grievance they experienced yesterday and today,

More exact than the fogs.

Look up! On the way to pursuing bird nests encircled by clouds,

A snake freshly shed its deceased hide,

Yet unfortunately paralyzed swollen in the shrubs.

It is struggling to recover from its carelessly broken backbone

Due to the female snake's excessive defiance in copulation.

Its up-rising tongue is   aiming at the floating clouds,

Hissing.

Look up! The floating clouds are always at the utmost altitudes.

Yesterday they just floated over the treetops,

Today they are floating over the horizon

And over an autistic person just approaching the horizon,

In front of the singular scenes he just came upon.

The floating clouds and he are stooping

In places unknown to people, vomiting

A big pile of things more grotesque than imagined,

And a big pile of stone-like tasteless apparition

Enveloped in the bosom for years.

浮云绘

向上看　那些浮云扔下的行踪
惊飞了一只飞鸟一天的行程
和一只蚂蚁人所不见的一生

只有飞翔才能抵达的悬崖上
那些没有泥土也能生长的柏树
松树和无名的藤蔓
只有风知道它云雾中凝结的露珠
以及昨天和今天　它所经历的
比云雾更确切的委屈

向上看　在追逐被浮云所包围的鸟巢的道路上
一条蛇蜕掉了已经死去的皮囊
却不幸臃肿地瘫痪在草丛里
它在努力修复交配时　由于母蛇过分的反抗
而不慎折断的脊背
向上升腾的蛇芯子　对着浮云
吱吱作响

向上看　那些浮云总是在最高处
昨天它们刚刚飘过树梢

今天它们正飘过地平线

和刚刚接近地平线的一名自闭症患者

在他刚刚发现的奇异景观面前

浮云和他正佝偻着腰身

在人所不知的地方　呕吐着

一大堆比想象更古怪的事情

和在胸口上装了多年的

一大堆石头一样淡然无味的鬼

Beauty of Silence

I imitate a certain beast

In bawling by craning the neck,

And birds in the trees are becoming increasingly hushed.

The leaves trembled off trees, as if birds got shot unfortunately,

Are slowly and somewhat hesitatingly falling from great heights

And having themselves deeply concealed in the bushes.

寂静之美

我模仿着某种野兽的样子
引颈高叫着
而树丛中的鸟愈发沉默

被震落的树叶　仿佛不幸中弹的鸟儿
缓慢而略带迟疑地从高处飘落下去
在草丛里深深隐藏起来

Beauty of Confrontation

I'm not a crude naturalist,

Namely, I'm not a bee or a brook.

I'm not one taking advantage of flowering or flooding phases

To approach the aim of the world on the brim of collapse.

I'm one holding a spade in hands,

I'm one holding a handful of glass shards in hands,

I'm one holding a spade glistening due to long use,

Walking and stopping, all along selecting and measuring places,

All along digging the land and its silence in distant places.

I spread a handful of glass shards in old yards and barren terrain

Like spreading a handful of seeds on a non-identified star.

I dig on the sands un-cultivated by earthworms,

I dig on the saline-alkali land un-eroded by tree roots,

I dig on wastelands on the seashore lapped against by the waves.

I'm, under the starry sky, in places where

The dark makes the world more impenetrable or unfathomable.

Sometimes I lose patience with the digging,

Spread glass shards like spreading a handful of seeds.

Eventually, I'm digging inside of myself.

In my body, in areas life and death accommodate in secret,

I have dug out another starry sky

With bizarre debris and trash belonging to this starry sky,

The debris hard to be tamed as glass shards,

For no other purpose but to witness with my naked eyes,

Between it and the stellar river overhead,

The harmony hard to clarify like cotton fiber

Or the beauty of confrontation.

对峙之美

我不是一个简陋的自然主义者

就是说我不是一只蜜蜂　或者一条河流

我不是赶着花期或汛期

去接近世界濒临崩溃的目标的人

我是手握铁镐的人

我是手握一把碎玻璃的人

我是手握一把因为使用太久而闪闪发亮的铁镐

走走停停　一直在选择和丈量地方

一直在挖掘大地和它在远方的沉默的人

我在旧宅院和荒凉地带撒下一把碎玻璃

像在未经识别的恒星上撒下一把种子

我在没有被蚯蚓耕耘过的沙地上挖掘

我在没有被树根腐蚀过的盐碱地上挖掘

我在波涛拍打过的海边荒地上挖掘

我在星空下　在黑暗

使世界变得更加深沉或莫测的地方

有时我失去了挖掘的耐心

像撒下一把种子一样撒下碎玻璃

最终　我也在自己之中挖掘

在身体中　在生与死已暗中通融的地带
我挖掘出另一个星空
和属于该星空的那些奇异的碎屑和垃圾
那些仿佛碎玻璃一样难以驯服的碎片
不为别的　只为目睹
它与头顶的星空之河
那种棉絮般难以澄清的默契
或者对峙之美

Notes:

【1】 MuUs（毛乌素）：Mu Us, from Mongolian language meaning "foul water", also known as the Mu Us Desert or Mu Us Sandy Land（MUSL 毛乌素沙地），is located in the northwestern fringe of the East Asian monsoon region and is sensitive to climate variability and global changes. The desert is characterized by mobile, semi-fixed and fixed sand dunes. It, as one of the severe desertification areas in China, is adjacent to the north of loess plateau in Shaanxi Province, in other words, Yulin city is located in the southern margin of the Mu Us Desert. Running through the southern margin of Mu Us, a main branch of the Yellow River Wudinghe River is in the Hekouzhen-Longmen Reach（河口镇—龙门河段）. The Mu Us Sandy Land has undergone climate changes and shifts in human activities driven by a series of ecological restoration projects in recent decades. Happily, the desert is on the way to becoming an oasis.

【2】 The Yellow River（黄河）：The Yellow River or Huang He is the second-longest river in China after the Yangtze River at 5,464 kilometers, with a basin area of about 752,443 square kilometers. The headwaters of this mighty river lie in Kunlun Mountains in northwestern Qinghai Province. Originating in the Bayan Har Mountains（巴颜喀拉山脉）in Qinghai Province in western China, it flows through nine provinces and autonomous regions: Qinghai, Sichuan, Gansu, Ningxia Hui autonomous region, Inner Mongolia autonomous region, Shanxi, Shaanxi, Henan and Shandong all the way from west to east to the Bohai Sea（渤海）.
The Yellow River is the cradle of Chinese civilization, the spiritual home of the Chinese people. The Chinese people call it the "Mother River". It is the waters of the river and its spirit that nurture the whole Chinese nation. For thousands of years, this river has been admired by literary giants, artists, as well as by the common people. The Yellow River is not just several letters, nor is it just the name of a yellow-ochre-colored river. It bears special significance: the symbol of the Chinese nation, the spirit of the Chinese people and more importantly, civilization itself.

【3】Mediterranean（地中海）: The name Mediterranean is derived from the Latin Mediterraneus, meaning "inland" or "in the middle of the land"（from medius, "middle" and terra "land"）.

Mediterranean Sea, an intercontinental sea that stretches from the Atlantic Ocean（大西洋）on the west to Asia on the east and separates Europe from Africa. It has often been called the incubator of Western civilization. This ancient "sea between the lands" occupies a deep, elongated, and almost landlocked irregular depression lying between latitudes 30°N and 46° N and longitudes 5°50′ W and 36° E.

The western extremity of the Mediterranean Sea connects with the Atlantic Ocean by the narrow and shallow channel of the Strait of Gibraltar（直布罗陀海峡）, which is roughly 8 miles（13 kilometers）wide at its narrowest point; and the depth of the sill, or submarine ridge separating the Atlantic from the Alboran Sea（阿尔沃兰海）, is about 1,050 feet（320 metres）. To the northeast the Mediterranean is connected with the Black Sea（黑海）through the Dardanelles［达达尼尔海峡 with a sill depth of 230 feet（70 metres）］, the Sea of Marmara, and the strait of the Bosporus［sill depth of about 300 feet（90 metres）］. To the southeast it is connected with the Red Sea（红海）by the Suez Canal（苏伊士运河）.

In oceanography, it is sometimes called the Eurafrican Mediterranean or the European Mediterranean Sea to distinguish it from Mediterranean seas elsewhere. It was an important route for merchants and travelers of ancient times that allowed for trade and cultural exchange between emergent peoples of the region. The history of the Mediterranean region is crucial to understanding the origins and development of many modern societies. For the three quarters of the globe, the Mediterranean Sea is similarly the uniting element and the centre of world history.

【4】Poseidon（海神波塞冬）. Poseidon, Greek God of the Sea was one of the most powerful of all of the gods in Greek mythology. He was one of the 12 Olympian gods and goddesses who held court on Mount Olympus—the mountain of the gods. Poseidon is the son of Cronos and Rhea（克洛诺斯和瑞亚）, and brother to Zeus（宙斯）, Hades（哈得斯）, Demeter（得墨忒尔）, Hestia（赫斯提）, and Hera（和赫拉）.

【5】Confucius（or Kong Zi 孔子）: Confucius (551 BCE -479 BCE)

was China's most famous teacher, philosopher, and political theorist, whose ideas have profoundly influenced the civilizations of China and other East Asian countries. *The Analects*（*Lun Yu* 《论语》）is a collection of Confucius' sayings gathered in a single text, which is one of the pillars of Chinese culture and has been widely read across the centuries. The only other comparable book in Western Culture is *the Bible*.

【6】Mount Tai（泰山）：Mount Tai or Taishan Mountain, the first of the Five Sacred Mountains, is located in the central part of Shandong Province, within the precincts of Jinan（济南）, Licheng（历城）and Tai'an（泰安）, covering an area of 426 square kilometers. Its circumference is 80 kilometers. The highest peak of this mountain range about 1545 meters above sea level, lies within Tai'an city. Mount Tai abounds in lofty peaks, deep valleys and rare cultural relics of the old days. Rising abruptly above the North China Plain in central Shandong Province, Mount Tai is one of the Five Sacred Mountains of China. Taishan Mountain was once called Mt. Dai（泰岳）or Mt. Daizong（岱宗山）before. It was renamed Taishan Mountain during the Spring and Autumn Period（春秋时期）. In 1987, UNESCO listed Mount Tai as the World Natural and Cultural Heritage.

It lies in the civilized land of the ancient states of Qi and Lu（齐国、鲁国）with the Yellow River on the north and the sea on the east. A famous saying goes, "Scaling Taishan Mountain makes one feel superior to the whole world"（登泰山而小天下）, as it creates a feeling of regal dignity and imperial majesty. Many romantic scholars of old considered it a great treat to express their sentiments on top of Taishan Mountain. The mountain is an early birthplace of China's ancient civilization and the area around was one of ancient China's political, economic and cultural centers. Since ancient times Taishan Mountain has been hailed as the "most sublime of the five mountains". Apart from its impressive height and ancient culture, the reason is probably that men have deliberately deified it.

Historical records show that a total of 72 emperors of bygone dynasties, from the first Qin Emperor Shihuang（秦始皇）onward, have made sacrifices to Taishan Mountain. This association with feudalism has earned the mountain a widespread fame. Nowadays, after repeated renovations, Mt. Tai has become more enchanting than ever before.

Translating Yan An

At last, my translation of Yan An's poems is coming to an end. I remember, in the winter of 2009, I first began to read through Yan An's two poetry anthologies—*The Land in Coexistence with the Spider* and *The City of Toys*. As I read on, I began to have an increasingly deeper understanding of Yan An. On the first day morning of the Chinese lunar new year, 2012, a sudden impulse of talking of Yan An occurred to me. I quickly spread out the paper and jotted down the title *Talking of Yan An*. Then without intentional planning, without deliberate arrangement, I finished writing the article fluently at one sitting for over four hours. Through repeated pondering and improving, I was finally able to spell out all my impressions and feelings about Yan An's poems, ending up with a smooth and coherent copy of *Talking of Yan An.* Before long, out of fascination and veneration for his poems, another idea dawned on me—Translating Yan An.

However, I didn't actually start the translation until the end of March of 2014, when I didn't expect Yan An would be honored with the award of the Sixth Lu Xun Literature Prize for his poetry in a few months' time. And my translation turned out to be nearly ten years on and off, a far more painstaking and prolonged time than I had ever expected.

At first, I tried to accomplish the poem rendering chore as soon as possible, but soon I found my such efforts in vain. I thought translating a poet's poems is just like standing on the shoulders of a giant, quite an easy errand. Yet on the contrary, translating Yan An's poems is like being indulged into a trap or being decoyed into a labyrinth, like stepping on a fascinating, misleading and endless adventure. Every poem's translation needs repetitious reading, comprehending and digesting, needs repetitious weighing phrases, creating sentences and rearranging or restructuring sentences so as to restore the original poems' linguistic expressions and ideological conceptions or have necessary innovative interpretation of the original poems. What's more, Yan An is a prolific poet. In recent years, he has had new poems composed almost every year and even poem anthologies published, such as *Sorting Out Stones*, *The Blue Kids' Seven Summers*, *The Naturalist's Mansion*... His new poem anthologies impacted me, ignited me and inspired me to go on with the translation.

In order that I can accurately comprehend and interpret each poem's implications, and can more thoroughly get acquainted with and figure out the poet himself, I find chances to get involved with the poet Yan An, and at times share my English versions with him for comments. However, on many occasions, he falls in absolute silence, as though he suddenly remembers something, and abruptly sets about writing poems, so engrossed as to have left me in suffocating silence, totally ignorant of my presence. This often reminds me of William Wordsworth's definition of poetry:"*Poetry is spontaneous overflow of powerful feelings; it takes its origin from emotion recollected in tranquility.*" Yan An, a down-to-earth poet, makes his life fully packed with poetry, and makes his daily life teemed with colors, verve and charm through his poetic speech. The American poet of free verse Walt Whitman seems to refer to Yan An in a poem entitled *Song of Myself* —

I am the poet of the Body and I am the poet of the Soul,

The pleasures of heaven are with me and

the pains of hell are with me,

The first I graft and increase upon myself,

the latter I translate into a new tongue.

...

When doing the translation, I found: Spider, this image word, now and then appears in Yan An's poetry, spitting out gossamer thread and weaving webs, putting intricate ideas generalized and connected, and putting delicate emotional textures well–arranged and coupled. Poetry, like a spider, starts from the core to expand out to create "dot-line-face" gold-brocaded verses.

Uppermost poems like this definitely require the absolute silent concentration of the poet Yan An with billowy emotions to carry out the composition. This silence is not the dead silence, but a stability easily hinting us of proverbs like: Still waters run deep and still stones stand steady, and also reminding us of the majestic high-rise mountains—the Qinling Mountains. The Qinling Mountains, serenely partitions and delineates the China's territory, puts it well-arranged and well-proportioned in interlacing or crisscrossing patterns, fascinating and charming. Yan An portrays the concealed profoundness and unfathomed connotation of the boulders on the Qinling Mountains in his poems. The silence of recluse type in Yan An's poetry is occasionally broken by an abrupt-flying giant bird and a raven howling to the moon, as though a pebble had been thrown into the poetry pond, splashing and rippling the water. Such a start of surprise enlivens poetry, entrusting poetry with vitality and spiritualism, exhibiting charms vivid; Such a start of surprise activates poetry, allowing poetry to have rhythms and beats, setting rhymes flowing; Such a start of surprise also affects the readers' hearts, allowing the readers' imagination to have wings, together with the poet, to perceive a panoramic image of the cosmos, to be aware of the mystery of thought and mind, and to be content in infinite awareness of and in compassionate introspection upon the harmonious relationship between the sentient beings and the world.

Apart from his observation of gigantic birds, enormous fish and the transcendental images of the fish Kun transforming into the bird Peng (roc), Yan An also, in a low-profile stance, looks at the solitary birds in low places, and even draws our attention to more minute, negligible life form: a tiny anemone flower concealed in a corner of the unfathomable universe. An idea of becoming a fish surfaced in his poetic heart heaving like the sea, and he went deep down the ocean and gazed at life's most primitive, most instinctive and secretive germination and its incredible romance and twining. From fish to the enormous fish Kun, from Kun to the gigantic bird Peng, from the microcosmic to the macrocosmic, the poet Yan An utterly throws himself into the vast sea, soars into the vast sky, cruises along, composing poetry at leisure, undoubtedly displaying the uninhibited airs of Du Fu, who is known as the poetry saint of the Tang Dynasty, composing verses so apropos, chanting alone at ease. From fish to Kun, from Kun to Peng, from microscopic to macroscopic, the poet Yan An thoroughly sees through the human rune and resolves the cryptogram of life, creates the most macroscopic realm in the most microscopic form of language and pursues the possibility of mankind from limitation to infinitude.

In the course of translation, I can't help but associate Yan An's poetry with the world-class poets':

> *In your soul is perched a spider.*
> *The shape of the spider*
> *Is the shape of your soul.*
> *The way the spider spits out silk is the way that*
> *Your soul is intricately entangled with certain phantom.*
> *...*

The spider spits out silk, filament after filament, and inescapably dwells deep in the soul of the poet Yan An. I can't help wondering if the spider that perched in the poet Yan An's heart also lingered in Walt Whitman's heart:

> *A noiseless patient spider,*
> *I noticed it stood isolated in a small headland,*
> *Notice how it surveyed around the vast emptiness,*
> *It forth filament, filament, filament, out of itself,*
> *Continuously from the spindles on the wire, accelerate the speed tirelessly.*
> *And you — O my soul, where you stand,*
> *Being surrounded, isolated in the ocean of the limitless space,*
> *Ceaselessly musing, adventure, projection, seeking the spheres,*
> *You need until erecting bridge, till the ductile,*
> *Till the gossamer thread you fling catch somewhere, O my soul!*

The spider in total isolation in Walt Whitman's poem seemed to be the spider trapped in a rotting crevice in Yan An's poem. It experienced double tortures of daydreaming torment and disturbing conceptions, and exceedingly suffered extreme emptiness and profound solitude, eventually sinking into serene concentration and meditation, ending up being a noiseless and patient spider, and in the elapsing time with light and darkness together waxing and waning, began to explore, to seek space, and contrive for a breakthrough, silently awaiting the light to appear.

In the poem *Birds Also Like Low Places,* we can sense the humility and affection of the poet Yan An. This kind of warmth is also found in the poem by an American female lyrical poet, one of the pioneers of Imagist Poetry, Emily Dickinson, honored as forefather of modern American poetry: *A BIRD Came Down the Walk*

> *A Bird came down the Walk—*
> *He did not know I saw—*
> *He bit an Angleworm in halves*
> *And ate the fellow, raw.*
> *And then he drank a Dew*
> *From a convenient Grass—*
> *And then hopped sidewise to the Wall*
> *To Let a Beetle pass—*
> *He glanced with rapid eyes*
> *That hurried all around—*
> *They looked like frightened Beads, I thought—*
> *He stirred his Velvet Head*
> *Like one in danger, Cautious,*

I offered him a Crumb

And he unrolled his feathers

And rowed him softer home—

Than Oars divide the Ocean,

Too silver for a seam

Or Butterflies, off Banks of Noon

Leap, plashless as they swim.

A poem *Four A.M.* (*The hour from night to day / The hour from side to side / The hour for those past thirty...*) by Wislawa Szymborska, winner of the 1996 Nobel Prize for Literature, Polish poet and translator, makes me involuntarily recall the poet Yan An, who placed the bathing maiden at three o'clock in the morning, a more previous and secluded moment:

Early morning, at three o'clock,

Water splashing sounds arise,

Her pure, greasy and aromatic body,

A glaring beam of white gleam.

Water around hopping and leaping,

Purely white, freshly bright,

Stirring up plumes of misty fog.

...

Or:

Early morning, at three o'clock,

Water splashing resounds,

Her body arises,

Delicate, fragrant

Dazzling, brilliant.

Hopping and dancing is the water around

White, bright

Hazy, mazy.

...

Poets are deeply familiar with the truth that familiarity breeds contempt while distance fosters beauty. Therefore, they often keep a certain distance in time and space from the world, watching the external surroundings while looking internally with introspection as an uninvolved bystander, to sketch out the real world from the perspective of peace and ease.

Yan An's observation and contemplation of the real world are also reflected in his poems. In *The City of Toys, "The children's faces are half given by parents/And half made of glass and another substance like that"*. It reminds me of the poem *Peckin* by the American poet Sheldon Alan Silverstein:

The saddest thing I ever did see

Was a woodpecker peckin'at a plastic tree.

He looks at me, and "Friend" says he,

"Things ain't as sweet as they used to be."

In Sheldon Alan Silverstein's poem, the woodpecker can no longer find the initial taste of trees. The woodpecker is actually pecking at a plastic tree. The situation of woodpecker easily sets me dwelling on the miserable plight of mankind, who is the culprit of all this, depicted in Sheldon Alan Silverstein's another poem *Examination*:

> *I went to the doctor*
> *He reached down my throat,*
> *He pulled out a shoe*
> *And a little toy boat,*
> *He pulled out a skate*
> *And a bicycle seat,*
> *And said, "Be more careful*
> *About what you eat."*

The modern is downright a society deluged with plastic, glass and artificial materials like that, a society in which there's emptiness widely spreading, devoid of authenticity and simplicity. "Return to the primitivism of living things, return to the actual essence of life; let all living things return to the life habitat for natural multiplication, let humans return to the original ecological spiritual homestead." That is the shared plea of great poets!

When I was translating Yan An's poem *The Mediterranean*, another poem *Ruined Homes* flashed into my mind quite naturally, which was written by a poet named Nikola Madzirov, who was born in Macedonia of the former Yugoslavia, from a refugee family during the Balkan Wars. The poems both end up with brief and to-the-point complaining assertions and forceful denouncements for the miserable world.

The Mediterranean

> ...

Today I'll write about the Mediterranean,
Which is a tomb in time,
Is Europe's blood, is one basin of cold blood
With Homer's and gods' incisors knocked out,
And with the time's incisors knocked out.

Ruined Homes

> ...

Our ruined homes were a move of the world,
of the memory, of the memory.

(Translated in English by Graham and Peggy Reid)

This kind of connection makes me assured: Torments in the world are globally widespread, the poets in the world are the most affectionate group, the poems in the world are the most serene sayings of wisdom.

I can't help but associate Yan An's poetry with the world-class poets'. Especially with my increasing in-depth comprehension of Yan An and Yan An's poetry, I grew to hold the notion that Yan An is wholly on a par with world-class poets, or to some extent, Yan An's poetry will be even slightly superior. This may be because Yan An has been immersed in the wisdom of the oriental boundless cosmology for too long ever since childhood. It is because Yan An has been exposed to the mysterious and profound folk styles in northern Shaanxi for too long ever since childhood. Towers, temples, jade, witches, and incense, which are typical of the oriental homeland, are haunting in the poems of Yan An, creating the most primitive religious atmospheres like ritual worshiping and praying on the Loess Plateau. From "*The Birth of Water*", the source of life, to "*Confucius Must Have Seen the Sea*" depicting the sage's heart boundless like the sea, from chanting the "*Messenger's Hymns*" to eulogizing Mao Zedong's boundless magnitude of mind like the sky in the "*Absolute High Landscape*", we are obliged to believe that Yan An's poetry are innately endowed with the spiritual code of the Chinese nation, which has been passed down for thousands of years and is thoroughly imbued with upright spirits of rainbow-like majesty, overflowing with divinity and glorification. In Yan An's poems, the quietness in northern Shaanxi is persistently brewing the magnificent momentum like the Hukou Cataract torrents pouring and booming loud; In the poetry of Yan An, the oriental wisdom distinctively starts up the magnificent rhythms of radiance with the sun overwhelmingly beaming down, the splashing water-vapor and the sun rays interrelating brilliantly, brightening the soul, moistening the life, and revealing the oriental charm:

> *Absolute great landscape was born*
> *Half a century ago,*
> *The endless earth was brilliant like fire,*
> *On the earth, a life*
> *More majestic than water,*
> *A man named Mao Zedong was walking in Shanbei*
> *Like a fire dragon walking amid the flame.*
> *When a nation sunken in tribulations,*
> *He was walking through the flame for it*

For it he enjoyed the serenity in the flame.

This sort of oriental charm of sonorous resonance is rarely found in poetry of other countries. Yan An is the bellwether of poetry at the legendary absolute height, manifesting overwhelming passions by means of concise poems. I can affirm that the absolute height of spiritual space must have been brought forth through numerous dialogues and strifes between the poet Yan An and the absolute height of physical space. The absolute height of spiritual space must have leisurely arisen in Yan An's heart in the wake of the poet having experienced heavy powerful impacts from the Loess Plateau one after another. The absolute height of spiritual space must have sprouted up after the poet Yan An having experienced repeated toppling and annihilation by the towering Qinling Mountains. At this absolute spiritual height, the poet Yan An uses the method of drawing big pictures out of small facts, as if waving flags to call out the heroic declaration of the great man Mao Zedong, *"Have confidence in living a life for two hundred years, have courage in fighting the waters for three thousand miles"*. At this absolute spiritual height, the poet Yan An overlooks the mighty Yellow River to explore the source of the vast Chinese civilization. At this absolute spiritual height, the poet Yan An holds his breath and holds to his bosom the grand northern Shaanxi from a historical perspective, expressing the heroic spirits of the city Yan'an. At this absolute spiritual height, the poet Yan An looks at the land of three Qin kingdoms, walks across the Qin land of eight hundred miles, heartily displaying the eternal romance of Chang'an (the present name Xi'an) , the ancient capital city for thirteen dynasties in the history of China. Yan An was born in northern Shaanxi, worked in Yan'an, and lives in Xi'an; As the

Chinese character "An" implies, Yan An is a poet with a quiet endowment. He takes advantage of his tranquil meditation and wisdom to utter witty words and sonorous sentences. Yan An's poetry are intriguing, unique, and are related to the alpine background, on which he depends. They are related to the holy culture he grew up in. They are related to the clear-cut coordinates of geography, to the crisscrossing cultural coordinates and to the crystal-clear spiritual coordinates he built in the depths of his mind. I can't help but associate Yan An's poetry with the world-class poets' ...

Through my practical translation, I instinctively feel that the relationship between the poet, the poems, and the translator is mysterious. This three-in-one state of harmony needs to be attained by a specific and unique translator, and to be relied on a freshly-rendered version bred with painstaking efforts. Lucky enough, as a translator, I am endowed with such unique traits of a poet as being simple and complicated. Being simple is simply to hold fast to the truth while being complicated is solely to fly free with imagination. Translating Yan An's poetry allows me to have a sort of psychological experience similar to that of poets when writing poetry. Once in a while, I experienced pangs of puzzlement, frustration and torment, in the meantime I also felt acute senses of achievement, pleasure and satisfaction. I'm intoxicated in recreating mysterious images in the target language, and in setting off a chemical reaction among the readers of the target language.

Translation is the key to the expansion of both the world and the ego. Translation is not only having the superficial mission of the linguistic transition of poems completed, but having the poet's poetry life span lengthened, let alone having the translator's visions broadened and even his spiritual realms elevated.

In the face of the silent poetry, in the face of silent Yan An, in the face of China's most secretive spiritual nobility, as a translator, I must treat the poetic code of mystery with awe in heart by way of the same tranquility, standing on the giant's shoulders to look at the multi-dimensional absolute high landscapes of time and space!

Dante condemned all Dante's translations in advance; Goethe emphasized that poetry is not translatable, but the translation of poetry is absolutely necessary. The author of the *Translator's Mission*, Walter Benjamin said, "*Each work completes itself in translation. Good works are calling for translation and can withstand translation.*" Yan An's poetry is calling for translation, calling for me predestined, calling for me aptly to be willingly devoted to a translation for nearly ten years.

In order to further improve the translation, I took the initiative to interact with some modern western scholars, such as Robin Gilbank.

Robin Gilbank, from England, has been in Xi'an for over ten years. He used to teach in Northwest University and is currently teaching in Xi Jing University. In recent years, Mr. Robin Gilbank and Professor Hu Zongfeng have co-translated many literary works of Shaanxi writers and started the mission of connecting Chinese and Western cultures.

From my correspondence with him in 2014, I could already see Robin Gilbank's preference for the poetry of Yan An, and my English versions of *The Deserted Lawnmower* and *A Contract with the Wolf-god* were to his particular liking.

Another example is the American scholar Hank Weaver, who once taught in Yan'an Middle School, even used the word "choppy" (*undulating*) to describe his overall feelings about Yan An's poetry. It seems as if Yan

An's poetry of vehemence brought tremendous astonishment to him. The impact was so intense that Hank Weaver, who was already in his sixties, even recalled the contemporary American rhythm and blues singer Alicia Keys' song *P.O.W.* He even offered the entire lyrics to me. From our correspondence, we can see Yan An's poem *The Statue and the City* is Hank Weaver's favorite.

At the onset of finalizing the translation of Yan An's poems, I would like to express my sincere gratitude to Robin Gilbank, a doctor of Medieval English Literature, and Hank Weaver, an American scholar. Likewise, I would like to thank my family and friends for their hugely great support and help. Thanks to you all!

翻 译 阎 安

文世龙

终于，阎安诗歌的翻译将要接近尾声。记得二〇〇九年冬天，我第一次真正开始拜读阎安的两部诗集《与蜘蛛同在的大地》《玩具城》，边读边对阎安形成了越来越新的认识。二〇一二年大年初一的早晨，我突然萌发了写写阎安的冲动，于是铺展纸张写出标题《话说阎安》。没有刻意的构思，没有刻意的布局，一早上四个多小时就洋洋洒洒写出了初稿；而后经过反复推敲完善，将我对阎安及阎安诗歌的全部认识和感悟拓展开来付诸笔端，《话说阎安》就这样诞生了。不久，出于对阎安诗歌的迷恋与尊崇，又一个念头在心头萌发——翻译阎安。

真正着手翻译阎安诗歌是在二〇一四年三月底，当时没想到，几个月后，他的诗集将获得第六届鲁迅文学奖。而实际的翻译工作，断断续续，竟然绵延了近十年之久，漫长而艰辛。

起初，我试图尽快完成这项工作，但很快发现我的努力是徒劳的。原以为翻译诗人的诗就像站在巨人的肩膀上，应该说是一件很轻松的事情；然而恰恰相反，翻译阎安的诗歌就像慢慢沉溺在陷阱里或者被不断引诱到迷宫里一样，情不自禁地沉沦其中，越陷越深，不能自拔，仿佛踏上一场令人着迷但又极易令人误入歧途的没完没了的冒险之旅。每一首诗的翻译需要反反复复的研读、理解、内化，需要反反复复的斟酌、遣词、造句，需要句式的重新编排与组合，以还原诗歌原有的语言表达、思想意境，或者对原诗歌进行必要的创新解读。

加之，阎安是个多产的诗人，近年来，几乎每年都有新的诗集问世，《整理石头》《蓝孩子的七个夏天》《自然主义者的庄园》……这些新的诗集总是冲击我、燃烧我、激发我，使我在翻译之路上越走越远。

为了准确地理解和翻译诗歌的寓意，更好地熟悉和读懂诗人，我找到了更多接触阎安的机会，不时地与他分享交流译作。与他在一起的很多场合，我发现他时不时会陷入极度的静默当中，刹那间好像想起什么，开始动笔挥洒诗句；全神贯注的他，常常将我置于令人窒息的平静当中，全然忘却了我的存在。这不由得让我想起英国浪漫主义诗人威廉·华兹华斯对诗歌的定义："诗是强烈情感的自然流露。它起源于在平静中回忆起来的情感。"阎安，这个纯粹的诗人，将诗行充斥生命的角角落落，他用诗意的语汇将生活的斑斓和神韵泼墨而出。美国自由体诗人沃尔特·惠特曼的诗《自我之歌》仿佛表达了诗人阎安的心声——

> 我是肉体的诗人，也是灵魂的诗人
>
> 我占有天堂的愉快，也占有地狱的苦痛
>
> 前者我把它嫁接在自己身上使它增殖
>
> 后者我把它翻译成一种新的语言
>
> …………

在翻译诗歌的过程中，我发现："蜘蛛"，这一意象词语，时不时会在阎安的诗歌当中吐丝结网，把错综复杂的思想头绪归纳串联，把细腻如织的情感纹理排列组合；诗歌像蜘蛛一般从核心向四周铺展开来，呈现出"点—线—面"连缀而成的锦绣诗文。

这样一首首上乘的精品诗文确实需要诗人阎安具有澎湃中秉持极度静默的定力。这种静默不是死寂，而是静水流深、安若磐石般的稳审，让人一下子想到巍峨的山脉——秦岭。秦岭，静静地分隔构架华夏版图的阡陌纵横和万千风情。秦岭山上的巨石在阎安的诗歌中重现其秘而不宣的深邃和深不可测的底蕴。阎安的诗歌中这种静若隐士的寂默也偶尔会被一飞冲天的巨鸟、对月长啸的乌鸦打破，仿佛一块块鹅卵石霎时间投进诗歌的池塘，溅起水花，激起涟漪。这一激灵活化了诗歌，让诗歌有了能量、有了灵气，气韵生动；这一激灵激活了诗歌，让诗歌有了律动、有了节奏，意韵流动；这一激灵也波及读者的心灵，让读者的想象力有了翅膀，与诗人一起感知时空和宇宙的错综全景，觉知思想和心灵的神秘浩渺，安住于对众生与世界无限慈悲的静默观照中。

除了关照巨鸟、大鱼及鲲化鹏的超然意象外，阎安也放下姿态平视那些低矮处形单影只的小鸟，关注更加渺小微细的、被人们忽略的微乎其微的生命——隐秘在深不可测的宇宙一隅之地的一朵小小的海葵花。诗人阎安澎湃如海的心头绽放出变成一条鱼的构想，潜入深海之渊，静观生命最原始最本能的秘而不露的萌动和不可思议的缠绵。从鱼到鲲、从鲲到鹏、从微观到宏观，诗人阎安完全把自我投身于浩渺的大海，腾飞于无垠的天宇，游弋于作诗咏歌，优哉游哉，不免显露出唐代"诗圣"之称的杜甫"赋诗歌句稳，不免自长吟"的自由气象；从鱼到鲲、从鲲到鹏、从微观到宏观，诗人阎安似勘破人类符文、开解生命密码，将语言以最微观的形态来创造最宏观的境界，探寻人类从局限到无量的可能性。

在翻译的过程中，情不自禁，我会把阎安的诗歌和世界级诗人联想在一起。

你的灵魂里盘踞着蜘蛛

蜘蛛的形状

就是你的灵魂的形状

蜘蛛抽丝的样子

就是你的灵魂与某个幻影藕断丝连的样子

…………

蜘蛛吐出一缕一缕的丝，防不胜防地蜗居在诗人阎安的灵魂深处。我不禁怀疑，盘踞在诗人阎安心头的蜘蛛也曾挥之不去地萦绕在沃尔特·惠特曼的心头：

> 一只无声的坚忍的蜘蛛，
>
> 我看出它在一个小小的海洲上和四面隔绝，
>
> 我看出它怎样向空阔的四周去探险，
>
> 它从自己的体内散出一缕一缕一缕的丝来，
>
> 永远散着——永不疲倦地忙迫着。
>
> 而你，啊，我的灵魂哟，在你所处的地方，
>
> 周围为无限的空间的海洋所隔绝，
>
> 你不断地在冥想、冒险、探索，寻觅地区以便
>
> 使这些海洋连接起来，
>
> 直到你需要的桥梁做成，直到你下定了你柔韧的铁锚，
>
> 直到你放出的游丝挂住了什么地方，啊，我的灵魂哟！

（李野光译）

沃尔特·惠特曼那身处四面隔绝地方的蜘蛛仿佛就是阎安被困在腐朽的缝隙里的蜘蛛，经历了想入非非的痛苦和妄念杂飞的缠缚的双重折磨，饱受了极端的寂寞和深刻的孤独的淬炼，终于沉入入定和冥想，成为一只无声的坚忍的蜘蛛，在光明与黑暗消长的光阴更迭中开始了探险、寻觅空间、谋略突围，静默地等待光明莅临。

在诗歌《鸟也喜欢低矮的地方》中，我们可以感受到诗人阎安的谦卑和慈爱。这种温情在美国抒情女诗人、意象派诗歌的先驱之一、被誉为美国现代派诗歌的鼻祖艾米莉·狄金森的诗歌《一只鸟沿小径走来》中也会发现：

一只小鸟沿小径起来——

它不知道我在瞧——

它把一条蚯蚓啄成两段

再把这家伙生着吃掉。

然后从近旁的草叶上

吞饮下一颗露水珠——

又向墙根，侧身一跳

给一只甲虫让路——

它用受惊吓的珠子般

滴溜溜转的眼睛——

急促地看了看前后左右——

像个遇险人，小心

抖了抖它天鹅的头

我给它点面包屑

它却张开翅膀，划动着

飞了回去，轻捷

胜过在海上划桨

银光里不见缝隙

胜过蝴蝶午时从岸边跃起

游泳，却没有浪花溅激

（江枫译）

一九九六年诺贝尔文学奖获得者、波兰女诗人兼翻译家维斯瓦娃·辛波丝卡的一首诗《凌晨四点》（白天与黑夜交接的那个小时／辗转与反侧之间的那个小时／年过三十之人的那个小时……）让我不由自主地想起诗人阎安将《沐浴的少女》置身于凌晨三点，这一更加置前、更加隐秘的时刻：

凌晨三时

水声响起

她净腻而芳香的身体

一道耀眼的白光

四周的水跳跃起来

洁白，鲜亮

激起阵阵迷蒙的雾

…………

　　或许，诗人们深谙"熟悉生轻蔑，距离产生美"的道理，所以常常与这个世界保持时间和空间的距离，以旁观者的姿态观望对镜、反观内心，以清净自在的视角白描本真的现实世界。

　　对现实世界的抨击和关注时常体现在阎安的诗歌当中。当翻译阎安的《玩具城》"孩子们的脸一边是父母给的／一边是玻璃和另一种类似的材料做的"时，我不由得想起美国诗人谢尔·希尔弗斯坦的《啄》：

　　这是我见过最忧伤的事了

　　一只啄木鸟在啄一棵塑料树。

　　它看了看我说，"朋友呀"，

　　"这树木再也没有以前的味道了。"

（冯默谌译）

　　在谢尔·希尔弗斯坦的诗中，啄木鸟再也找不到树木以前的味道了，啄木鸟竟然在啄一棵塑料树。啄木鸟的境遇让我又不由自主地想到诗人谢尔·希尔弗斯坦在另一首诗歌《检查》里所描述的这一切的罪魁祸首人类的悲哀窘况：

我去看医生

他把手伸到了我的喉咙里，

从里边拽出了一只鞋子

还有一艘玩具船，

他还从中拉出了一双溜冰鞋

以及一个自行车座，

他叮嘱道，"你要留心

你所进食的事物"。

（冯默谌译）

现代社会简直是一个充斥塑料、玻璃等虚饰材料的社会，矫饰伪行、空虚蔓延的社会，少了真实少了质朴。"回归生物的原始状态，回归生命的本来面目，让万物生灵回归自然生息的生命家园，让人类回归原生态的精神家园。"这是诗人共同的呼唤！

而当翻译阎安的诗歌《地中海》的时候，我又不由自主地想到生于南斯拉夫的马其顿，出身于一个巴尔干战争难民家庭的诗人尼古拉·马兹洛夫的诗歌《毁掉的家园》。这两首诗歌的结尾简明扼要、直截了当，类似牢骚满腹的断言，对这个世界苦难的铿锵控诉：

…………

今天我要写到的地中海

是一个时间中的坟墓

是欧洲的血　是磕掉了荷马和诸神门牙

也磕掉了时间门牙的一盆子冷血

——《地中海》

我们毁掉的家园是一个移动的世界

> *移动的记忆*
>
> *移动的记忆。*

——《毁掉的家园》

（冯默谌译）

而这种关联让我更确信一点：世界上的苦难是遍及全球的，世界上的诗人是最温情最慈悲的群体，世界上的诗歌是最静默的智慧箴言！

情不自禁，我会把阎安的诗歌和世界级诗人联想在一起，特别是随着我对阎安的深入了解，对阎安诗歌的深入理解，我越来越觉得阎安完全可以和世界级诗人比肩——某种程度上，阎安的诗歌会更高一筹。这也许是因为阎安自小以来在东方博大宇宙观的智慧海洋里浸染得太久太久，是因为阎安自小以来在陕北神秘厚重的民风中熏陶得太久太久。东方家园独具的塔、庙、玉、巫、香在阎安的诗中缭绕荡漾，营造出黄土高原上一幕幕最为原始、最具仪式感的崇拜和祷告的宗教气场。从生命之源"水的诞辰"到"孔子一定见过海"的圣人那海洋般的博大胸臆，从吟诵"使者的赞美诗"到颂扬"绝对高度上的风景"中毛泽东那天宇般的广阔胸怀，我们不得不相信，阎安的诗文秉有华夏民族几千年来一脉相承的精神密码，气贯长虹，以神性和颂扬的气韵荡漾开来。阎安的诗文中，陕北的宁静生生不息地酝酿着势如壶口瀑布般的轰然倾泻的磅礴气势；阎安的诗文中，东方的般若秒秒分明地启动着灿若阳光般的灌顶如注的喷薄律动，飞溅的水汽和普照的阳光霓虹并灿，透亮了心灵，润泽了生命，彰显出东方神韵：

> 绝对伟大的风景诞生于
>
> 半个世纪前
>
> 无边的土地辉煌如火
>
> 土地之上，一个比水

更磅礴的生命

一个名叫毛泽东的人行走陕北

如卷火之龙行走于火焰的中心

在一个民族沉入苦难之后

他为它而穿越火焰

他为它而享受火焰中的宁静

　　这种黄钟大吕般洪亮的东方神韵在其他国家的诗歌中是罕见的，阎安在传说中的绝对高度上独领风骚，以简洁的诗文掀起波澜壮阔、激情澎湃。我敢断言，这种精神空间上的绝对高度，肯定是诗人阎安与物理空间上绝对高度的一次次的对话对决而生发的；这种精神空间上的绝对高度，肯定是诗人阎安经受黄土高原厚重雄浑的一次次的冲撞冲击在心中悠然突兀隆现的；这种精神空间上的绝对高度，肯定是诗人阎安承受过秦岭山脉扶摇巍峨的一次次的倾覆湮泯在心中顷刻破土腾踔的。在这种精神的绝对高度上，诗人阎安凭借以小见大的方式挥旗呐喊出伟人毛泽东的豪迈宣言："自信人生二百年，会当水击三千里"；在这种精神的绝对高度上，诗人阎安俯视浩浩滔天的黄河水，探寻浩浩荡荡的华夏文明的源头；在这种精神的绝对高度上，诗人阎安屏气凝神以历史纵横的视角收揽大陕北于胸怀，抒发英雄延安之气概；在这种精神的绝对高度上，诗人阎安望眼三秦大地，游走八百里秦川，纵情挥洒十三朝古都长安的千古风流。阎安生于陕北、缘系延安、身居西安；一个"安"字的交融，契合了诗人阎安特有的气质，他以安然静默的定慧吐露字字珠玑、句句铿锵。阎安诗歌散发出来的耐人寻味、卓尔不群，和他依靠的巍峨背景有关，和他浸染的神圣文化有关，和他在心灵深处构筑的脉络分明的地理坐标、纵横交错的文化坐标、清澈剔透的精神坐标有关。情不自禁，我会把阎安的诗歌和世界级诗人联想在一起……

　　通过翻译实践，冥冥中我觉得：诗人、作品、译者三者关系玄妙，这种三位一体的和融状态是需要特定的独一无二的译者倾力达成的，是依托呕心沥血孕育的鲜活译本达成的。所幸的是，作为译者的我秉有诗人既简单又复杂的特质。思想的简单，可以使我更纯粹地坚守； 思维的复杂，可以使我更自由地放飞想象力。翻译阎安的诗歌，让我体验到一种类似诗人创作诗歌时的心路历程，偶尔会感到困惑、沮丧和压力带来的痛楚，同时也可以感受到强烈的成就感、愉悦感和满足感。我陶醉于将诗歌在目标语中再现奇异的图景，在目标语的读者中掀起一番化学反应。

翻译是世界和自我同时获得拓展。翻译不仅仅完成了诗歌的语言转换这样表层的使命，而且延续了诗人诗歌的生命，更拓宽了译者的视野，甚至提升了译者的心灵境界。

面对缄默始终的诗歌，面对安然静默的阎安，面对中国最隐秘的精神贵族，作为译者的我必须用相同的神闲气定来敬畏蕴藏玄妙的诗意密码，站在巨人的肩膀上，望眼多维度的时空上绝对高度上的风景！

但丁预先责难了一切但丁作品的翻译；歌德强调诗歌是不可翻译的，但诗歌的翻译又是绝对必要的。而《译者的任务》作者瓦尔特·本雅明说："每一部作品在翻译中才完成了自己，好的作品都是在召唤翻译的，也经得起翻译的。"阎安的诗歌就是召唤翻译的，召唤缘定三生的我，召唤恰如其分的我，情不自禁，长达十年之久。

为了使译文精益求精，我曾多次主动与外籍友人们交流沟通。比如罗宾·吉尔班克先生。

罗宾·吉尔班克先生，英国人，在西安已有十多年。他曾在西北大学任教，现任教于西京大学。近几年，罗宾·吉尔班克与胡宗峰教授合译了许多陕西籍作家的文学作品，做起了构架中西文化桥梁的工作。从我与罗宾·吉尔班克先生二〇一四年的书信中，可以看出他对阎安诗歌的喜爱，而且他更偏爱我英译诗歌中的《荒凉的割草机》和《与狼神签约》。

再比如，美国学者汉克·维沃。汉克·维沃，曾在延安中学任教，他竟然用"choppy"一词来描述自己对阎安诗歌的整体感受，看来阎安诗歌中澎湃汹涌、排山倒海般的气势冲撞到他了，其冲击的程度甚至让六十多岁的汉克·维沃联想到美国当代节奏布鲁斯歌手艾莉西亚·凯斯的歌曲*P.O.W.*，他居然还将整个歌词与我分享。在交流中他说，他最喜欢的是阎安的诗歌《雕像与城》。

与西方文人的一次次的互动交流、一次次的反馈和评论，仿佛一粒粒精神资粮为我蓄势储能，推我一步步顺势而为完成阎安诗歌翻译的终极冲刺。在结束阎安诗歌翻译的此刻，我再次感谢英国中世纪英语文学博士罗宾·吉尔班克！感谢美国学者汉克·维沃！感谢家人和友人们的诸多支持与帮助！谢谢大家！